Ruby River Ruckus

ROD SCURLOCK

authorHOUSE®

AuthorHouse™
1663 Liberty Drive
Bloomington, IN 47403
www.authorhouse.com
Phone: 1 (800) 839-8640

Published by AuthorHouse   06/19/2015

ISBN: 978-1-5049-1636-3 (sc)
ISBN: 978-1-5049-1635-6 (e)

Library of Congress Control Number: 2015908990

Print information available on the last page.

This book is printed on acid-free paper.

This book is dedicated to a WWII hero who sailed on the same kind of ship I did, who lived through some of the fiercest battles of the war, including Iwo Jima, and is one of my dearest friends, George Menhorn. George, you asked for this book and here it is.

# CHAPTER ONE

The pounding on the door finally soaked into his brain. His head ached and no sane thought was coming through. For a time, he couldn't think where he was. Nothing looked familiar.

Oh, yeah. He and the boys had celebrated a little last night. Slim had wrangled a bottle somewhere, and they had talked him into coming down to the bunkhouse and helping them empty it. Well, it was good to let off a little steam after the long haul getting the cattle here, and then getting the ranch ready to go. A little relaxation was called for.

He pulled back the covers from his bunk, and lowered his feet to the floor, then sat up gingerly. He pulled on his Levis and rose, then, walked slowly to the door. When he opened it, Slim was standing on the porch.

Bart looked at the tall puncher. "Slim, what in the blue blazes is goin' on? You're makin' enough racket to scare all the cattle back to Texas."

"Sorry, Boss. I just looked across the river and there's a wagon comin'. Thought yuh oughta know."

"All right, Slim, build a fire, will you, and put on some coffee. I'll get dressed."

By the time he had shaved and donned his clothes, he could hear the wagon grind to a halt out front, the horses stomping and snorting. As he came into the kitchen, Slim came in from outside.

"Boss, thar's a wagon out thar' with a load o' pots and pans thet'd outfit an army"

"Yeah, I told Al to take Carmelita in to town and get what we needed. She was supposed to get with Ruby and decide what we had to have."

"Well, yew may know how t' manage a herd o' cattle, but when yuh jest let two women go 'thout a bridle on 'em - whooee!"

Al came in with a load of pots and pans. "Where do you want these?"

"Put them there on the table. Is that all of them?"

Slim laughed. "Boss, thet's only what was on the first wagon! The warehouse in the back of the store jest about fell in, with nothin' left in it."

Bart grinned, ruefully. "All right, Slim, go help him haul in the rest. I'll try to make room for it."

Al and Slim made several more trips from the wagons, piling the table full of dishes, pots and pans. Then Al went out and brought in a load of rolls of cloth.

Bart looked at him. "What's this?"

"They will be curtains. Feller, they're goin' to make a civilian out of you before you're through." He chuckled and went to the stove and poured himself a cup of coffee. "You didn't put any limit on the spending, and I got outvoted every time I tried to say something."

"I didn't intend to put a price on it, but what in the world do they need all of this for? The whole table is stacked full. I can understand a skillet, and maybe a mush kettle or two, but all of this?"

"Now you're beginning to get the idea of what it's like to be married. You see that sweet young thing with those big eyes and curving lips and think I want that for the rest of my life, and then you start to realize that she doesn't necessarily want to squat down in front of a campfire with a skillet in her hand and cook your meal every night. Before long, you'll start getting soft, and think about the nice things she prepares for you every day, and then the nice soft bed without rocks poking you in the ribs, and you'll start to think maybe this is a better life. Maybe I can put up with a few pots and pans."

"I can see Carmelita has got you hornswoggled already. You used to be a good cowhand! Before long, I probably can't get a day's work out of you."

"I notice you haven't turned down any of her meals."

"Well, let's go down and surround one of 'em now, and get to work."

When they had finished eating, Bart asked all of the hands to come into the big house for a few minutes. When they were all seated, Bart went to his desk and pulled out a roll of bills. He looked at the two riders who had been with them on the trail drive. "Boys, we appreciate your help and it's time you were getting paid. You've been good hands, but I'm sure your boss is wanting to see you back. We'd like to keep you, and if you want to stay, the job is yours. At any rate, here's your wages."

The two took the proffered money, and after shaking hands all around, took their leave and left.

After they had gone, Bart looked at Slim. "Well, it's just the three of us now. With the mountains and the river surrounding the place and all the good feed, it shouldn't be too hard to keep the cattle corralled until we can get some fencing done. Before long, we'll have a herd put together that'll take a dozen men to work it. You'll have a whole crew of men to boss around."

"I hope they'll be as hard workin', easy to get along with, and downright top hands as the crew I have now."

"I just wonder every day why I keep the crew you're bossing now. It's ornery, lazy, shiftless, and just no good, so Slim, why don't you take your horse and your crew, the team and wagon, and your good nature, down to the flat this side of the river. Start digging some post holes along the road and then on the west side from the hills to the river, about a quarter of a mile down. We'll put a holding pasture there. I'll go in to town today and get some fencing, and then I'll go help Al cut some posts. I'll see if I can pick up another hand or two while I'm in town. Al, hang tough a few minutes. I want to talk to you."

Slim put on his Stetson. "Shore 'nuff, Boss. Jest remember, any gold I find is mine."

After Slim left, Bart went into the cook shack and retrieved a couple of cups of coffee, and came back and handed Al one of them.

"Al, you're a full partner in this outfit, and you've been sleeping in the bunkhouse with Slim and the other boys. I know I started out with the office in the second bedroom here in the big house, and I've got the other one. I think what we will do to start with is get enough lumber to build another bunkhouse down by the corrals. The boys'll be happier there away from the big house and we'll make the old bunkhouse an office.

"I wasn't going to do this so soon, but I can tell that the way you and Carmelita are carrying on, it won't be long until you'll be needing other quarters. You can move into the second bedroom right away, and you and she can live there after you're married. Then, when we can get some more money put away, we'll build another house for you. How does that sound to you?"

"It sounds great, Bart, but I still say that this thing should be your ranch, and I'll be a good hand. You put this whole thing together, and I just helped where I could. Carmelita and I have been talking some along those lines, but haven't made any specific plans."

"No, you've more than earned it, and I need you as a partner. We're goin' to have the biggest ranch in Montana before we're through. Now, go cut some poles and I'll see you tomorrow. I'm goin' to stay in town tonight."

Al laughed. "All right, tell her 'hello' for me!"

Dusty was across the corral when Bart opened the door. That trusty horse came trotting over, looking for an oat handout or something similar, that Bart usually had for him. Bart laughed. "You are a beggar of the first degree." He reached into his pocket and pulled out an apple. Slicing it in half with his knife, he fed it to the horse, getting a nuzzle in response. "All right, you had your snack, now let's get up to the big city."

After the horse was saddled and he was on board, Bart rode over to the edge of the bench and looked down at his land below him. It was a beautiful sight. The lush green valley, covered with the bountiful grass, was set off by the blue river running through the middle, and it stretched out away from him until it reached the base of the foothills on to the east. He could see the heifers grazing across the water, and below him, he could see Slim digging post holes for the holding-pasture fence. He gave a sigh of contentment. Everything had gone smoothly since they had arrived with the cattle a couple of months ago.

The cattle had settled down, Al and Slim had established a daily routine, and he had been able to get loose to go see Ruby at least once a week. Ruby, with her shoulder-length, dark brown, wavy hair, bright brown eyes, her beautiful rosy lips that were almost always curved up in a smile. She was tall for a girl, with a slim, willowy body that filled her dress out in just the right proportions. He had come to know what a wonderful person she was, also. She was the most important thing in his life, anymore.

Their usual visits included a night at the opera house, followed by a meal at the café, or sometimes just a walk down by the creek. Many times, they were with Ginny and Buster, and he and Buster had become close friends.

He stopped the daydreaming, nudged Dusty into a lope, and headed for Alder Gulch.

James Gray was sweeping off the haberdashery porch as Bart dismounted and tied Dusty to the hitch rail. "Howdy, Bart. How are you?"

"Pretty good, Mr. Gray. Is Ruby around?"

"She's upstairs. Before you go see her, would you take a minute and come into the office?"

Gray's office was situated in the back of the store. He indicated a chair. "Sit down, Bart. I need to talk to you."

Bart took a chair. "What's up?"

"Bart, we have been seeing a bunch of rough- looking gents around lately. One was in yesterday. He walked around the store looking at everything, which isn't so unusual, but he kept peering over his shoulder, looking at me, and it gave me the chills. I was sure he was going to rob me, and, thankfully, Ginny and Buster came in looking for Ruby. The man kept watching us and finally gave up and left without buying anything. There have been several others much like him lately that no one knows. They don't appear to be miners, or cattlemen, just drifters."

"Have any of them caused any trouble?"

"No, not to my knowledge, but they have all of the businessmen worried. As you know, we don't have any law in the country any more since we ran the sheriff out of town. Not that he was any good to keep law and order - he was worse than the crooks."

"Well, I guess there isn't anything we can do until they start something. I'll keep an eye peeled while I'm in town." He left the office and went upstairs to find Ruby.

She came to the door when he knocked, and when she saw who it was, flew into his arms and kissed him. "Oh, Bart, I'm glad you came in. I've been so lonesome for you."

"Me, too, Sweetheart." He looked at the piles of cloth around the room. "What are you doing?"

"Making curtains for Ginny's house when they get married. She's hoping it will be soon. They're buying the old Sampson house. He died a little while ago, and Mrs. Sampson is selling the house."

"Yeah, I saw the roll of cloth that you sent with Al." He grinned. "How are you going to be able to look out our windows and see if the cows are all right, if they're all covered up with cloth?"

She chucked him under the chin. "Oh, that's no problem. You'll be sleeping in the barn and can look out any time!"

He picked her up, whirled her around the room, set her back down, and kissed her. "Sassy women are an abomination!"

Buster and Ginny were waiting at the front of the opera house when Bart and Ruby arrived. Buster's sandy-red hair contrasted with Ginny's light-brown hair, and though he was not much more than average height, his body was like a stone mountain, solid as a piece of steel. This made a real contrast with Ginny's short, slim stature. In spite of this difference, they made an attractive couple. Both had laugh wrinkles around their eyes, and ready smiles. Bart cottoned to them again, as he had every time they met.

They found seats toward the back of the room, and settled down to watch the show. Bart had trouble keeping up with the performance of the elocutionist. James Gray's comments about the toughs that were coming in to town kept forcing their way into his thoughts. They had cleaned the crooked sheriff and his gang out of the country, and now it looked like another bunch was coming in to take their place!

After the show was over, the four went to the café for some pie and coffee. Ruby kept looking at Bart and finally poked him on the shoulder. "Hey, does our company bore you? You're awful quiet tonight."

"I'm sorry. I just can't help thinking about what your dad was saying about the drifters coming in to town. Have you seen them, Buster?"

"There are a few around lately that I don't recognize. I've shoed horses for a couple of 'em. They were pretty tight-lipped. I asked 'em where they hailed from and neither would open up. They're kind of shifty- eyed, too. I wouldn't trust them any further than I could throw a longhorn steer."

"Well, maybe I'm seeing trouble where there isn't any. At any rate, I came in to hire a couple of hands. Have you seen anyone looking for work?"

Ruby put her hands on her hips and pretended a pout. "I thought you came to town to see me!"

"Not unless you can build a quarter-mile of fence a day."

Buster laughed. "Well, if Ruby doesn't take the job, I know of one young feller that could use some work. Come by in the morning, and I'll go with you to see him."

The next morning, after they had eaten, Buster led Bart to a rooming house on the next street down the hill from the main thoroughfare. He knocked on the door and an elderly lady answered. "Can I help you?"

Buster said. "Yes, Mrs. Austin. We need to see Edmond. Is he home?"

"Yes. I'll call him."

Soon, a young man came to the door. Buster introduced them. "Bart, this is Edmond Grant - Bart Madison.

Bart shook his hand. It was twice the size of his own hand, and his grip was like a vise. The young man stood over six feet tall, and looked as big as a barn, and all muscle. His eyes were friendly and looked ready to smile.

"I'm glad to meet you, Edmond. I'm looking for a hand out at my ranch on Ruby River. Would you be interested?"

"My poke is gettin' pretty low, and Mrs. Austin is kind of stretching to keep me here. I am interested. I like to eat. If you want me, I'm your new hand."

"Good. Do you know anyone else who might be wanting some work?"

"My budddy, Shorty. He's about in the same fix as I am."

"All right, Edmond, bring him with you and we'll give you both a try." He gave him directions for getting to the ranch.

"We'll be there in the morning. Oh, and most folks call me 'Bear'."

Bart shook Buster's hand after they returned to the main street. "Thanks, Buster. He looks like he isn't afraid of work. I keep thinking of what Mr. Gray said. Do you think we have a problem with all the tramps coming to town?"

"Don't know. If it continues, we sure could have. The ones that I've seen all were packing guns, some of 'em had 'em tied down. I sure wouldn't want it to get back to what it was before we moved the sheriff and all his gang out of town. Well, I'd better get back to work."

"All right, Buster. See you next trip."

Ruby was in the store when Bart arrived. He walked over to where she was arranging some Stetson hats. "Have you got one of those that fits me?"

"No, your head is too big for any of these." She laughed. "We have some nice women's hats that are probably just about right."

"You're never going to let me forget that, are you? I've got to head back to the ranch. Have you time for a cup of coffee?"

"Let's have it here. Go grab a chair on the back porch and I'll bring the coffee."

When she came out with the coffee and set a cup in front of him, he reached over and pulled her down on his lap. "Ruby, when can we set the date? My big house over there is getting awful lonesome."

"Bart, give me a little more time. I'm as anxious as you are, but I want to be sure my parents are all right with it before I leave them."

CHAPTER TWO

The ring of the hammer against the steel sounded for several blocks down the street. Sweat from the heat of the forge, and from the exertion, sent rivulets of moisture down his forehead, as Buster gave the final strokes to the axle he was making for the mine wagon. He used more steel in it than the original, given the heavy loads of ore they were hauling with the loaded wagon.

Using his tongs and a short bar, he lowered the axle into the tub of cold water to temper the steel. A loud hissing erupted from the tub, and steam filled the room. When the metal had cooled, he lifted it out of the tub, and looked up as he leaned the axle against the wall.

Two hard-looking individuals stood in the open doorway. They had shifty eyes that took in every corner of the shop before looking back at Buster. Their clothes were dusty from apparently a long ride, each had a holstered gun tied down, and both had low-topped wide sombreros. Buster immediately felt a chill, looking at them. They were trouble.

"Can I help you gents?"

The man on the right stepped forward. "Yeah, my horse threw a shoe awhile back and the others are loose. Can you fix 'em?"

"Turn him loose in the corral in back. There's a small shed back there. You can throw your gear in there until you pick up your horse."

The man stared at Buster. His hand was hanging low over his gun. "I need him now."

"I'm in the middle of a rush job right now. I can have your horse done tomorrow morning, not before."

The man again stared at Buster. It looked like he was going to go for his gun, or that the two of them would be coming for him. Buster wished he had a gun, but that probably would mean the end for him. These were obviously gunmen, and likely quick on the draw. He reached over to the stand and picked up his tongs. He was going down fighting, if they did come for him!

The two continued to stare at him, and finally, the second man looked at his companion. "Come on, Slate, let's go down and get a drink. We can play cards 'til mornin'." They left the building and went around to the corral in back.

Buster set down the tongs and breathed a sigh of relief. He went back to setting the cooled axle in its hangers on the wagon. Bart's question came flooding back. It did seem like there were getting to be a lot of these hard cases in town, lately.

It was late when he finally finished installing the new axle, and tired as he was, he decided to stay and re-shoe the gunman's horse. He would just as soon they picked it up as soon as possible, and get out. They looked like twenty miles of bad road to him. The horse would be ready when the gunmen returned. He was big, and even brawny, he thought, and not afraid of any man, but he was no match for one of those forty-fives.

The freighter stood waiting near the counter as Jim Gray opened his safe and counted out two-hundred dollars. Jim closed the safe door, and returned to the counter. "Here you go, Mr. Gillespie. Two-hundred dollars. I thank you for helping get it all into the store. Have a good trip back, and I'll get next month's list started and mailed to you."

"Thank you, Mr. Gray. See you next month."

Gray walked to the front door with the man, and stood watching him as he climbed back in his wagon and drove off down the street. As he started to turn back into the store, he noticed three hard-looking strangers riding down the street past him. None of them looked over at him, and he watched them go until they stopped and tied up in front of the saloon. He had never seen any of them before. It seemed like there were getting to be a lot more of these strangers hanging around town lately. He walked back into the store and started unpacking his goods.

Stacking groceries on the shelves was a pain, and Jeff Pierson was tired. He would much rather be back over there by the big, round stove in the front corner of his store, telling tall tales with the rest of his cronies.

It was strange, he thought, some folks go to the saloons, drink, play cards, or just talk over a beer. Others hunt, fish, or just hang around town, and then there's this bunch. All of them have seen their working years gone by. They have no job, little income, and many live alone. They gather at his store, sit around the stove, and tell the same old stories over and over, and yet they all delight in doing it day after day. He would surely miss them if they didn't, however, and he enjoyed it himself.

Today, the subject was the number of owlhoots that had been coming through town. Jeff would have liked to sit in on that conversation. He had noticed it, also. He put the last can of tomatoes on the shelf, and was just walking toward the front of the store when Ike Barstow came in.

"Hello, Ike. How's the lumber business?"

"Slow. Need a few groceries. Some beans, flour, and some eggs, if you have 'em."

"Sure thing. Mrs. Holt was in this morning with a fresh batch. Want a whole dozen?"

"Yep"

"All right, hang on. I'll get 'em for you."

Jeff turned to the shelf where the eggs were stored, and as he did so, heard someone come in. He swung around to see who it was and saw a tough-looking stranger walk up behind Ike, grab him by the shoulders and shove him aside, then move up to the counter.

Jeff walked up. "Mister, you can just turn around and leave. You don't treat my customers like that in this store. Are you all right, Ike?"

The man leaned forward, putting both hands on the counter. "I'll treat anyone just like I want to. Get me a cud of chewin', and now!"

"You can go to hell in a handbasket. I'm not waiting on you."

The man stepped around the counter, took out a pistol, and as Jeff tried to fend him off, hit Jeff on the head with the barrel of his gun. Jeff groaned, and slid to the floor. The man walked on behind the counter, found his chewing tobacco, and walked back out of the store.

Ike and the others rushed over to help Jeff.

When Jim Gray heard what had happened at the store, he told Mabel, "This is the last straw. The town is just getting full of these outlaws. I'm going to call a town meeting and see what we can do about it."

"Who are you to call a meeting? You aren't the mayor, or anything."

"Someone has got to do it. This can't go on. This may be a rough and tough mining town, but we have to have some kind of law and order. We don't have a sheriff anymore."

Jim spent the rest of the day talking to business men, and setting up the meeting. That night, a bunch of grim men filed into his haberdashery.

Jim opened the meeting. "Gentlemen, you all know why we are here tonight. We have to do something about these toughs coming into town and raising all kinds of mischief. Anyone have any ideas?"

Jeff stood. "We don't have a sheriff anymore, since we got rid of the bad one. We could form a vigilante group like we had before."

That brought a swell of disapproval from the group. Jim said, "That was almost worse than the crooked sheriff. They did help get rid of him, but a certain element then carried things too far, and innocent people were getting hurt."

Harry Ferguson, owner of the barber shop, held up a hand. "Since, we don't have a sheriff anymore, and no organization to do anything, why don't we just make the bunch here tonight the town council, and make Jim the president? I say, everyone in favor raise their hand."

The vote was almost unanimous.

Jim said, "I don't know anything about running a town. Why don't you get someone else?"

There was a great deal of discussion, but in the end, Jim was still the president, and they voted to have meetings as needed, and annual elections to elect new council members and officers.

One member of the group said. "It's that bunch down at Robbers' Roost that's causin' all o' this. We should get our guns and go down there and clean 'em out!"

Jim said, "They are a bunch of professional gunmen. We'd just lose a lot of our group, and probably not hurt them much at all. Why don't we pool our money and go hire a professional sheriff? One who has a reputation for cleaning up a town. Then, maybe we can get this place cleaned out of these characters, and keep a peaceable, decent town to live in. We would have to pay a man like that quite a bit, but if he could do the job, it would be worth it."

"I still say we need to clean out that Roost bunch. They've got to be who's behind it all."

"Anybody else?" There was no response. "All right, give it some thought. I know a man who's familiar with that bunch. That cattleman down on the Ruby. He lives right across the river from 'em. I'll talk to him and see if he's seen anything. Let's meet again Monday. He comes up to see my daughter about every weekend. That'll give me time to see him and see what he knows. Give some thought to hiring a good sheriff."

Al hitched up the team and headed for the mountains for a load of poles that had been cut to size. Bart and Slim rode down to the holding pasture and started setting posts in the holes that Slim had dug earlier. Slim held the post upright until the holes were about half filled with dirt, and then began pounding the dirt with a small post to compact it. Bart shoveled in the dirt.

By noon, they had most of the posts in on the east side next to the road. When the last post on that side was in place, Bart said, "Let's call it a morning. I could use some grub."

"Boss, I sweat enough to drown a cat, and every drop was a piece of those hotcakes I had this mornin'. My stomach says it can't hold up my britches any longer if it don't get a refill. Let's go."

Al was back with a load of rails and already in the cook shack when they had the horses fed and came into the house.

Carmelita filled their plates and set them on the table as the three men sat down. "You eat up and I fill your plates again. I don't want no skinny cowboys on this ranch!"

After they had finished eating, Bart told Slim, "Slim, this afternoon, I want you to go to digging holes again on the far end of the pasture. That way, with a fence on both ends of the pasture, it'll hold the cattle for now, with the river on one side and the mountains on the other. They could get out up on the mountain side, or for that matter, could swim the river, but I don't think they will, with all the grass there. Al and I will start hanging rails on the posts we set this morning. We'll set posts on the other two sides some other time when we have more time.

About mid-afternoon, Slim came riding up, chasing the roan bull that he had led up from Texas. The bull was trying to get back to the herd and Slim was cutting him off from every move, until he had choused him clear up to where Bart and Al were working.

Bart looked up from the rail he was nailing. "Slim, what's wrong?"

"Boss, we gotta git rid o' this blasted cut-back! I cain't git any work done with him around."

"What's the matter?"

"He just follers me around all the time, comes right over and sticks his head down right where I'm diggin', and won't back off."

"Bart laughed. "Slim, he thinks you're his mother! You're the only family he knows, after leading him clear across this country and feeding him a nose-bag full of grain every day. He loves you!"

"Wal, he's goin' to git a dose o' lead poisonin' if he don't let me alone." Slim pushed the bull one more time with his horse, and then loped back to where he had been working, the bull following right behind him.

Bart and Al went back to their fence work. They set a gate in the middle of the stretch along the road, and when that was finished, they stopped to rest.

Bart raised his hand for quiet. "Al, do you hear that? Is that Slim hollering? It sounded like he hollered 'help', and then it sounded like laughing. Let's go look."

As they approached the end of the pasture where Slim was working, Bart could see Slim on the ground, and the bull standing over him. He spurred his horse over in that direction. He could see Slim was shirtless lying on the ground, with the bull straddling his body. Bart motioned to Al to hurry. "Al, that bull's got Slim down. He may be bad hurt."

Bart pulled his horse to a sliding halt, and jumped off to give Slim a hand. When he could get a good look at the puncher, he started to laugh.

Al came galloping up. He couldn't see Slim, but as he dismounted, he saw Bart laughing fit to be tied. Holding his sides and nearly rolling on the ground. "What are you laughin' at? Is Slim all right?"

Bart couldn't talk. He just pointed over to where Slim was lying, shirtless, on his back on the ground, and the big long-horned roan bull standing over him, holding Slim down with his nose and licking his belly, Slim alternately hollering 'help', and then pitching into a fit of uncontrollable laughter from the tickling. Slim would beat the bull on the head and then try to grab the horns to pull himself away, and the bull would push him back to the ground and start larruping him with his tongue again. Which would send Slim into another peal of helpless laughter.

Finally, when Bart could control his laughter, he walked over and chased the bull away and helped Slim to his feet.

"Slim, I know you love that bull, but I can't have you spending time with your pet. We've got work to do! We'll just have to put a salt-lick down here to take care of his needs." Then he broke out in a fit of laughter again.

Slim got red in the face and stomped back to where he was working. "I'll kill that cull-bait! If he sees another day, it'll be because I've died of wantin' his ornery hide spread out on a stretch-board and couldn't pull the trigger!"

The sun was closer to the top of the mountains to the west by the time Bart got through with the Saturday chores and could start for Virginia City. Ruby, Buster and Ginny would be there and waiting for him before he could get there. He was anxious to be with Ruby again. It was a week since he had seen her. He could hope that this time, they would be alone. He liked Buster and Ginny. They were a lot of fun, but it would be nice to have Ruby to himself this night.

It had become standard fare. When Saturday night came around, he rode the five miles up to Virginia City. Buster and Ginny, he and Ruby got together, took in a show at the Opera House, had something to eat at the café, and then said goodbye. Usually, there was little chance to have a private talk with Ruby. He was getting anxious to get their wedding plans settled. He knew that Ruby and Ginny spent a lot of time together, and talked about it a lot, but that left him kind of out in the cold.

Sometimes, when he stayed in town overnight, he could see Ruby the next morning, but when he had brought the subject up, Ruby held off setting a date because of something to do with her parents. Maybe they were reluctant to have her marry a rancher. He suspicioned that might be the case.

He tried to hide his disappointment when he came into Ruby's house and Buster and Ginny were there. Ruby reached up and kissed him. "You are late tonight. We were afraid something might have happened and you couldn't make it."

"No. I just couldn't get away any sooner. Can we still make the show?"

"We may miss the opening, but let's go now and see what we can."

Just as they were leaving, Jim Gray came into the room. "I thought I heard your voice, Bart. Could I talk to you a minute when you get back?"

"Sure."

After the show and they had eaten, he and Ruby said good night to Buster and Ginny and they returned to the store. When they entered the building, Jim Gray came down from upstairs. "Bart, come on up. I need to talk to you about something."

After they were seated in the living room, Jim Gray asked, "Bart, I don't know if you have noticed, but there are a lot more toughs, seedy-looking customers, and riffraff, in general, coming into town, and hanging around. Women and children are starting to feel unsafe walking down the streets, and store owners are having problems with 'em, as well.

"We held a meeting last week, trying to decide what to do about it. As you know, there is no law and order in town anymore, and even the old vigilante group has more or less dispersed since the old crooked sheriff left town. Most of the others feel that it's that bunch down at Robbers' Roost that're causing the trouble. I know that you're acquainted with some of them, and I wonder if you would be willing to look into it for us, and let us know if you think they're coming from there."

"That doesn't sound like what I do know of the bunch down there, but I'll ride over and look around, if you'd like."

"I know that this is an imposition on you, but we're having a town council meeting Monday night. Would it be possible for you to do it before then, and meet with us? The meeting will be here in the store at seven."

Bart hesitated for a minute. "All right, I'll see what I can do."

"Thanks, Bart. You don't know how much I appreciate that."

Bart thought to himself: I hope it's enough that you'll let me marry your daughter!

The sun was high in the heavens by the time Bart left Virginia City and was well on the road to Robber's Roost. As he passed Nevada City, he noticed a lot of activity around the first saloon, and more than usual around the rest of the small village.

Bart walked up to the door of the two-story Robber's Roost hotel. Sundance himself answered the door. He smiled. "Hello, stranger! What brings you to the wild side of the country?"

"Hello, Sundance. Wonder if I could have a few minutes?"

"Sure, come in, and have a seat."

"Sundance, please don't take offense at this. I just came from Virginia City. They are being overrun with toughs, and others, that are giving them problems. Many of the merchants think it must be an overflow from your establishment here. I told them it didn't sound like what I know of the folks here, and from what you told me before. They asked me to look into it, and I said I would come talk to you."

"I know people look on us as the very lowest of humanity, but as I told you before, what we're interested in is hibernation here. We don't want to make any waves that'd bring the law down here. We aren't above a robbery or two, that's how we make a livin', but not around here. We do go to Virginia City sometimes, but we make it a rule to behave while we're there, and not bring the law down on us. We do our business further away.

"I have noticed that Nevada City's filling up with a lot of characters like you're describing, however. I wouldn't be surprised if that's where your trouble is coming from. In fact, we'd like to see them out of here, so that they don't have the troops coming into the country to settle it down. In any case, it isn't us that's causing the problem."

"All right, Sundance. I was sure that was the case. I'll tell 'em. Thanks."

Bart was early as he rode up the hill to Virginia City. He reined the horse over to the hitch rail in front of the Gray Haberdashery, and dismounted. There were already several horses tied there. He climbed the steps to the covered porch and walked in the door.

Jim had just started the meeting. "Come in, Bart. We're just getting going on a few items. Since you're here, we'll make you the first on the agenda. What did you find out?"

"I talked to Sundance and one other down there. I'm convinced they are not the ones causing the problems."

Henry Ferguson shifted nervously for a bit. "How can you take their word for it? They're a bunch o' owlhoots down there. I wouldn't trust them for a minute." There was a general murmur of agreement throughout the gathering.

"I can't tell you to trust them. All I can say is that I believe Sundance to be telling the truth. As he told me, this is their hideout. They are outlaws and do a lot of things outside the law, but they come here to get away from the law, and their desire is to cause as little ruckus as possible, so as not to attract the law. My ranch is right across the river from them and I have had no trouble from them at all.

"Sundance did tell me that Nevada City is attracting a lot of unsavory characters. This may be where the trouble is coming from. At any rate, that's all I can tell you. You asked me to look around down there, and all I know is that I couldn't see anything amiss, and can only tell you what I believe."

Jim took the floor again. "Well, what's the feeling of the group? What do you want to do?"

Porter Slocum got to his feet and looked the group over. "We have been mulling this thing around now for about a week and we're no closer than we ever were. We don't have any law here and we don't want the vigilantes back again. They're as wild as the outlaws, most times, even though they did a good job gettin' rid of the crooked sheriff. Let's get down to cases and do something. I vote that we take Jim's suggestion. Pool our money, hire a really good sheriff, and keep him here. We need law and order the worst way. Our women and kids can't even walk down the street anymore!"

Jim looked each of them in the face. "Are you willing to put up whatever it takes to get one here, and will you stay with it to keep him here? Everybody willing to do this raise your hands."

Some of the hands rose immediately; others were raised reluctantly, but soon every hand was in the air.

Jim said. "All right. Every hand was up. We are all in agreement, and no one backs out later. Does anyone know of a good solid, and really tough, lawman that can handle that bunch of outlaws that are coming in?"

Bart sat their watching the crowd. He could see they didn't want to get involved, yet Jim held them to the subject, and kept them focused on the problem. His respect grew for Jim. He looked like a middle-aged business man, with little more problems than just managing his store, but as Bart watched the crowd's reaction to him, he began to appreciate the strength of the man. He was highly respected by everyone present, and was able to bring them to a meaningful conclusion.

Buster stood. "I heard of a sheriff down in Oklahoma City that cleaned up the town. It was just as bad, or maybe even worse, than we are. I don't know if he would come or not, but it would be a place to start. His name is George Menton. I don't think he is all that well known, but some of you may have heard of him."

Slocum grinned. "Maybe we could get Wyatt Earp, or Buffalo Bill."

Salty Borden looked over at Buster. "I've heard of Menton. There were a couple of drifters in my saloon a week or so ago talkin' about him. They said he was in Dodge, though. The way they were talkin', he's a whiz all right. I get a lot of business from these buzzards, but I'm with the rest of you. We need to clean 'em out if we're to have a decent town. I have a family, too. I say, let's see if we can get this guy, and I'm willing to put up my share of the cost."

Jim looked around the room. "Anyone else?"

There were no more suggestions. "All right, if there are no other ideas, let's have a vote. All in favor of sending someone to contact him, raise your hand."

Every hand was raised.

"Now, who can we send?"

Buster got to his feet. "I know who we must have to make the trip. It really isn't his fight, but all of you have been spending your life in your

17

stores and are in no shape to attempt such a trip. I don't have anyone to manage my shop. I'm all alone. I can't think of anyone else who has the stamina, who can get away, and who has the ability to convince the man to come. We need Bart Madison to do the job."

Bart jumped to his feet. "Buster! I've got a ranch to run. How could I go?"

"You have a partner down there who can take over, you just hired two new men, and old Slim could herd every cow you have, all by himself. I would trust you to do the job more than anyone I know."

"And I thought you were my friend!"

Jim Gray said, "Bart, I know it's a real imposition, but I would add one thing. It will be your problem as well when they get going in earnest. As they grow in numbers and get bolder, they'll be taking over the town as the last bunch did, and we'll be helpless to stop them. The women at your ranch will have the same problem when they come into town to shop. Their lives will be at risk, as well."

Bart studied at what had been said, and in addition, here was his future father-in-law talking about his daughter. "Let me have a couple of days to think about it. I'll talk it over with my partner." He didn't want to have to make the trip. They were still trying to get the ranch put together.

"We'll have money for your trip when you're ready, if you're willing to go."

When the meeting ended, Bart waited until Buster got ready to leave. He walked over and took his arm. "You're a great friend! The last thing in the world I want to do right now is make another big cross-country trip."

"I know, Bart, but this just has to be done, and when I look the crowd over, I don't see anyone else that can do the job. If this outfit gets too big, we're going to have the same mess we had a year ago, and it'll get down to your ranch, as well."

"Well, I'll talk it over with Al. Breakfast in the morning?"

"Six."

"All right. See you then."

Bart went back to his room. He lay, tossing and turning, going over the whole thing time and again. He never could come to a conclusion. He knew someone had to do it. There were more toughs hanging around every time he came to town. He even had to admit that it could be his problem down the line, even though the ranch was ten miles away. He just didn't want to leave right now, when the ranch was coming along so nicely.

What if he couldn't find this Menton? What if he wouldn't come with him? The whole trip would be wasted.

Buster had finished his coffee and was sitting waiting at a table in Susan's Café when Bart walked in.

"Hello, traitor. I hope that's poison in that cup!"

"I just knew who had the biggest line of bovine excrement in the group, and knew he would be the man to go." Buster grinned. "Seriously, I looked the bunch over. Most of them couldn't sit a saddle for a day, let alone a month-long trip. Beyond that, whoever goes is going to have to convince the man that he should come here to fight a bunch of outlaws. Why would a man do that? You're the only one I know, myself included, that might have a chance of getting the job done."

"Well, if Al and the crew don't have a problem with it, I guess I'd better. I can see where we all will have a real problem if it keeps on. You owe me a big one, though. Don't forget that."

After breakfast, he said good-bye to Buster, went to the livery and saddled his horse. He rode to the Gray Haberdashery where he tied the horse to the hitch rack and went into the store.

Ruby was selling some clothing to a lady, so Bart walked over to a chair behind the counter and sat down, watching. When Ruby finished the sale, she came back to the counter, made change for the woman, and after she was gone, turned to where Bart was sitting. "Well, hello, stranger. I thought maybe you weren't even going to come over and tell me good-bye."

"Your father has been keeping me pretty well occupied the last couple of days."

"Bart, he told me that they asked you to go find this sheriff. Are you going to go?"

"I don't know. I know someone has to. I'll talk to Al and the boys before I decide for sure. I have a lot to do down at the ranch. I know that everyone here is worked up about the strangers coming into town. We've had rough customers before. Are these any rougher than they were?"

"I don't want you to go. It could be dangerous.

Why can't they find someone else?"

"I told them I needed a couple of days to decide. They can wait that long. I'd better get going. I need to get some supplies back for Carmelita, or the boys'll go hungry this noon. I have two new men to get started this morning and I need to be there to get them going. I'm coming back up to tell your Dad of my decision. I'll see you then, probably tomorrow or the next day.

"All right, Bart. Please decide not to go. I love you."

"I love you, too. I'll see what the boys say about it. They have a stake in it, also."

Bart left, climbed aboard his horse, and rode toward the grocery store. Ruby watched until he was nearly out of sight.

She knew she was being foolish. Bart could handle himself as well as any man. She knew he was unhappy that she kept putting off the wedding date. She just felt she needed a little more time. She would be leaving the home she had known all of her life, her parents, and friends. Ruby! You're foolish! You are only going to be ten miles away - half a day's ride in the wagon. A lot of women move a lot further away than that when they marry.

She'd tell her dad she was leaving, and go see Ginny. Ginny always had a way of making things look brighter. Ginny, with her light-brown, curly hair and gray-blue eyes, always with a glint of humor in them. Ginny was pretty, and was always a favorite of the boys at the dances. She hardly ever had to sit a dance out. She was so lucky that Ginny was her best friend.

Ginny opened the door at her knock. "Oh, Ruby, I'm glad you came. I've been wanting to see you."

"Me, too, Gin. I'm up to here with stocking fabric. It gets so that I'm seeing print patterns in my sleep. Dad just got in a big shipment, and it's all I've done all day. I've about had it for one day."

"Let's go down to the café and get a cup of coffee. I've been cooped up here all day, too."

"That sounds great. I could use one, and a change of scenery."

The waitress came over after they had seated themselves at a table. "Hello, girls, what'll it be today?"

"Coffee and a roll"

"The same."

"The rolls are fresh. She just took them out of the oven."

Ginny slid her left arm across the table, and then left it lying there beside her cup. "Do you notice anything different about me?"

Ruby looked at her, from the top of her head and down as far as she could see. "Nope. You look just about like always. I'd recognize you anywhere."

Ginny raised her hand to her face and brushed it across her chin, and then lowered it to the table again. "Are you sure? Look again."

Ruby stood up and walked all around her and then sat down again. "No, you look just as devastating as ever. I can't see any difference."

"Ruby, take one more look."

"Oh, if you mean that ring on your finger that you have been waving in my face for an hour. Yes, I saw that." And she laughed, teasingly.

"Ruby Gray, I'm going to hit you. You saw it all the time!"

"It's beautiful"

"Buster gave it to me last night. He made it himself from a gold nugget he found in the creek."

"Have you set a date?"

"Not yet. We've talked about it some. What about you?"

"Not yet. Bart wants to get married right away, and I have been putting it off. I want to go a little slow."

"Don't you love him?"

"Oh, yes! Very much. I just want to be careful."

"Well, don't be too careful. If he goes on that trip, he'll be gone a long time. He might see some delightful senorita down in that southland. Then you'll get to be an old maid, and I'll bring all of my children over to see that old woman that lives all alone over her store."

"You make all that sound so good to look forward to."

"I was trying to. I don't want to be the only one big as a barn and packing one sniveling young one, with another hanging onto my skirts."

"Well, that doesn't sound a heck of a lot better."

Ginny laughed. "How many kids you have, and how soon, is up to you, but you had better lasso that cowboy, if you're going to have any. I've got to go. Let's finish up."

They paid the bill and left the café. They started up the wooden sidewalk toward the haberdashery, and Ginny said. "Let's go across the street. I saw a pair of arm-bands in the window of the gift shop the other day. I want to get a pair for Buster. He's always getting me something, and I want to do something for him. He has such wide shoulders, that he has to get shirts with sleeves too long to get one big enough for his shoulders. They're always getting in his way."

They went into the gift shop and Ginny bought a pair of arm-bands, and the clerk wrapped them for her. Ginny put them under her arm. "Ruby, come on up to Buster's shop with me. After I give these to him, I'll walk you home."

They walked on up the hill on the wooden sidewalk and turned the corner onto a gravel road leading up the hill to the right, where Buster had his blacksmith shop. They were nearly to the shop when two rough-looking men stepped out of an alleyway in front of them. One grabbed Ruby by the arm.

"Now, isn't this a pretty one. I think you and me should get better acquainted."

The other man was standing in front of Ginny, leering into her face. Ruby jerked her arm, but the man's grip was too strong and she couldn't pull loose. The man pulled her closer and leaned down, trying to kiss her. She slapped his face. "Let me go!"

"Now, isn't she the feisty one? Come here, sweetheart!" And he roughly jerked her toward him.

The other man grabbed the first one's arm. "Clive, let her alone. You know the boss said to not make any commotion yet. He wants to keep everything quiet. Let her go!"

"Not 'til I get a little kiss from this pretty!"

Ginny screamed, "Buster! Help! Buster!"

Buster came bursting out of his shop, looked around, and when he saw the two girls and the problem, came running down the hill.

The second outlaw grabbed the first. "Let go! There's trouble! Run!"

The first outlaw dropped Ruby's arm and the two ran down to the main street and turned up the hill.

Buster rushed down to where the girls were standing. "Are you two all right?"

Ruby brushed at her sleeve, as if to brush dirt from it. "Yes, thanks to you. Who were those two creatures?"

Buster switched his gaze to look down the hill to the main street. "They're a couple of the wild bunch that's been coming into town lately. Come on. I'll walk you both home, and then I've got to get back to the shop. I've got a wagon to fix for a man."

CHAPTER THREE

It was still pitch dark, and he could hear the wind howling around the corner of the house. Big, empty rooms just made the sound louder. He got out of bed, got dressed, and went down to the kitchen. The water jug was empty so he went out to the pump and filled it, then came back in and made a pot of coffee.

He couldn't sleep. His mind just kept going around on whether to go on the long ride to find that sheriff, or to stay and get the ranch put into shape. They had steers ready to market, and he hadn't yet made final arrangements to sell butchered beef. They did have the slaughterhouse done, and they were ready; he just hadn't contacted the merchants yet. He needed to do that before cold weather set in.

Bart sat mulling all of that over while drinking his coffee. Al came through the door. Bart looked up. "What are you doing up so early? Couldn't sleep, either?"

"No, I was sleeping like a baby, but you were thinking so hard it woke me up."

"As I said last night, they're pressuring me to go look for that sheriff. It's really the town's problem. We've got all we can handle here on the ranch. It's time to sell the steers. I haven't made arrangements to sell the meat, we haven't got all the hay in yet, and the holding pasture's still not built. I just can't leave the place. I just need to tell 'em I can't go."

"Well, partner, that's a decision you have to make, but as far as the ranch is concerned, Slim and I and the two new ones can handle that. I can go up and make arrangements for the meat sales. If you just don't want to go, that's for you to figger out."

"I think I'll go up and tell Jim Gray I just can't make it. Will you get the new men going on that holding fence with Slim?"

Al laughed. "Go ahead, Mother, take the trip if you feel like you should. We'll take care of your little pet. See you when you get back."

It was starting to rain by the time he reached the Alder Post Office. He stopped to see if he had any mail, and none being there, he got back on Buck and headed down the road. The rain was intermittent; at times it would just pour, and other times it was slack. He wished he had had the sense to pack his slicker.

He was soaked to the skin by the time he reached Virginia City. He reined in to the haberdashery, tied Buck to the hitch-rail and clomped in to the store.

Ruby was sitting behind the counter, talking to her dad. She looked around at Bart standing just inside the door, dripping water all over the place. "Dad, did you hear a squishing noise just then? It sounded like a wet puppy just came in and shook himself. Maybe I'd better go throw him out before he gets the hats wet."

She walked over and helped Bart out of his coat. "Where's your slicker? You're all wet."

"Wasn't raining when I left the ranch. I need to talk to your dad."

"Not until you get some of those wet clothes off."

Jim Gray came over. "Bart, come with me. We'll get you into some dry clothes."

As Bart was changing clothes, Jim asked him. "Did you hear about the run-in that Ginny and Ruby had with a couple of the toughs?"

"No, what happened?"

"They were walking up toward Buster's shop when they were stopped by a couple of these roughnecks. God only knows what would have happened to them if Buster had not come running. They've just got to be stopped!"

Bart sat staring at the floor, twisting his undershirt in his hands. Jim watched him for a while. "Bart, if you're trying to wring out the undershirt, I wish you'd do it somewhere else. You could cause a flood right here in the bedroom." He laughed. "Do you have a problem?"

"Jim, I came here to tell you that I wasn't going to make the trip, but I guess with this kind of thing happening, I had better go and see if I can find this sheriff."

When they came down the stairs, Ruby was sitting there, watching. As Bart came over to her, she stood, putting her hands alongside his face.

"You're going to go, aren't you? I can tell by the way you're looking that you're going!"

"I wasn't going to, but after what your dad told me about your run-in up by Buster's, I don't see any other way out of it."

"We weren't hurt."

"No, but you very well could have been if Buster hadn't come along."

"Bart, don't go. We'll get along."

He took her in his arms and held her tight for a long time, then raised her chin and kissed her. "I'm going to go. I'm going to get an early start and need to go back to the ranch and get things together. Tell Buster that if he doesn't look out for you and Ginny, I'll be after him with a twenty-foot-long whip." He kissed her once more and left.

Carmelita had just put the leftover food away when he walked into the kitchen. He poured himself a cup of coffee and sat down at the table. "Have you got any cold chicken legs? My stomach feels like I lost my teeth."

"You sit down and drink your coffee. Lots of good, hot food coming up. You go?"

"Yeah, I'll leave first thing in the mornin'. You can boss the ranch 'til I get back."

"I make these caballeros hustle. They be glad to see the major domo return. I'll have your trail grub ready. You take the pack horse?"

"No. I'm not going to take time for that. Just pack what jerky you can into my saddle bags. I'll live off the land, going."

"Por Dios! You be skinny as an old fence post! I feed you a lot of beans tonight!"

He rolled up some blankets and his slicker in a small tarp, and tied it behind his saddle, then brought an extra ration of oats over to the stall in front of Buck. "Partner, eat up. You'll be on a grass ration for a while. You and I are goin' to see some new country."

He went into the tack room and retrieved a few piggin' strings, some rifle shells and an extra dozen rounds of thirty-eight long-colt shells in a bag, and filled all the loops in his gun belt. After including a change of clothes, he felt like he was ready to travel.

# CHAPTER FOUR

Alder and Virginia City were both quiet when Bart rode through. He kept a steady pace throughout the day and arrived at the Madison River bridge as the strips of shadow grew longer and the sun sank over the horizon. He took a long breath as he reined Buck northeast along the river. He was on the way, come what would.

He found a spot on the lee side of a small hillock and dismounted. Buck walked over and nudged him as he was rolling out his soogans. "All right, partner, you're next." He unsaddled the horse, led him down to water for a drink, and then staked him out in some tall grass.

It had been a long day, he was tired and stiff. Why was he so stiff? He was used to riding. Maybe riding thirty miles or so had something to do with it. Well, there were a lot of thirty-mile days ahead. He just hoped that Borden was right, and Menton was actually in Dodge. He'd hate to have to make the trip for nothing.

He was up before the sun the next morning, had a cold breakfast, saddled Buck, and was on his way before the sun came up. He found a road that seemed to be going roughly in the direction he wanted to go, and followed it. Before long, he met a farmer in a wagon coming his way. He hailed him. "How far is it to the next town?"

"About twenty miles."

"Does this road come out at Bozeman? As I remember, there was a bridge there."

"No, Bozeman is another twenty up the river."

"How far if I just cut across country?"

"It'd probably be about thirty miles, but if you do that, you want to stay left of the mountains. If you get up in them, you'll be Christmas gettin' out. Just head about straight northeast and you'll about come out at Bozeman."

Bart thanked the man, turned Buck off the road, and cut across country in a northeasterly direction. He kept Buck at a fast mile-eating walk, stopped for a brief cold lunch, and continued onward until he could see the trees lining the Yellowstone in the distance.

As he approached the river, he rode down a steep hill and found a small stream coming out of the ground. A fairly good-sized pool was formed just below where the water was coming from the ground. Steam was coming up from the water.

Bart stopped Buck and dismounted. He walked over to the stream, knelt down and put his hand in the water. It was fairly hot. The sun was just going down, and he decided this was a good spot to spend the night. He hobbled Buck, had a quick meal, and thought he would take a bath. This would be all right. You didn't even have to heat the water.

Bart got out of his clothes and climbed down in the water. When he first sat down, it was so hot he almost jumped back out of the water, but in a little bit, he grew accustomed to the heat and he lay back, closed his eyes, and nearly went to sleep.

Suddenly, he heard some female laughter. He opened his eyes and saw two young women standing across the pond from him, laughing. Bart started to jump up to get his clothes which were out of reach on the bank, and then realized what he was doing and settled back in the water, trying to stir up a screen of mud. The girls, seeing what he was trying to do, laughed and came over to talk to him.

Bart was dying of embarrassment, and wanted to dive under the water. One of the girls pointed across the stream. "Oh, look, Sylvia, there are some men's clothes over on the other bank. They look like they just might fit my brother. I think I'll get them and take them home." Both girls burst into gales of laughter.

After what seemed like hours to Bart, one of the girls said, "Sorry, mister, we'll behave now. You really should get a bigger swimming suit." This brought another round of laughter, and the two girls left, talking and laughing as they went.

Bart felt like he was still blushing as he got out, dried off, retrieved his clothes, and hit the soogans.

Daylight found him in the saddle and crossing the river. Turning right as he entered town, he saw light in a building. It was a single-story, clapboard building, and a sign over the door said, 'Bozeman Café'. The morning was chilly, and a warm cup of coffee sounded good. It would wash down the cold jerky and hardtack. He tied Buck to the hitchrack in front, and walked in the door.

A young, blond lady came over to his table as he sat down. "Breakfast?"

"No, just a cup of coffee."

She returned with the coffee and set it on the table. "Out for a morning swim?"

He looked up. She was one of the girls at the pool. He turned red. She giggled, then turned and went back into the kitchen. Shortly, she returned with a plate of ham and eggs and set them down in front of him.

He didn't want to look up at her, but finally did. "I didn't order any breakfast."

"I know. We were mean to you, yesterday. Maybe this will help make it up to you. Breakfast is on the house."

He finished his meal, and as he got up to leave, she came out of the kitchen. "On a trip?"

"Yep."

"Will you be coming back this way?"

"Yep."

"She smiled. "Well if you want to take a swim then, we won't peek, I promise." She held out her hand to him. "Have a good trip."

He tried to smile as he shook her hand. "Thanks for the breakfast."

His face still felt red as he climbed into the saddle and started down the street.

The next two days went without a hitch. The road ran along the river almost all of the way. He could listen to the song of the water as it wound its way through the countryside. There was shade from the trees lining the river, and flocks of ducks rose as he passed, breaking the monotony of the ride.

He rode into the town of Big Timber late in the afternoon of the second day. He put Buck in the livery, and ordered an extra ration of oats for him. He also purchased a half sack of oats to tie behind the saddle. He could remember how much of the land a little further on was without much grass. Slim had said that a cow had to pack a lunch between clumps when they came through with the herd.

He arranged to sleep in the hay and paid the man for his and Buck's lodging.

The livery man was still sleeping when Bart rode out the next morning. He crossed the Yellowstone River bridge and turned east once more, making his way along the south side of the river. There was no road here, and he had to pick his way around tree clumps, small, sharp gullies, and other obstructions, but in general, the going was easy along the flat that sided the river.

Later that day, the river turned south and he had to ford it. It was much shallower here and there was no trouble making the crossing. Now, he was right in the middle of the Absaroka and Crow countries. He needed to thread the needle between the two. The Absaroka's lived in the mountain country and traveled mostly on foot; the Crow were primarily "hoss" Indians. Neither one would do him any good. He had had a run-in with the Absaroka's coming up from Texas.

He made his camp that night on the Shoshone River. He crossed to the other side. There was a good level spot there, and lots of grass for Buck. Cottonwood trees along the river provided wood for his fire, and everything looked rosy.

He built a small fire to cook some beans, which he found that Carmelita had spirited into his saddle bags. He had sprinkled them generously with small chunks of jerky to give them a little flavor. Hardtack and coffee filled out the menu. When he had finished eating, he went to the river and washed out his plate and put the dishes away. There was still a little daylight left, so he hobbled Buck and decided to walk upstream along the river to shake out a few kinks in his legs.

After walking about a mile, he decided he had gone far enough. A small knoll stood up just to the east of him, and he walked over to climb it and look around at the country. Just as he approached the summit, he heard the sound of horses. He flattened out, and crawled up to the summit.

When he reached it, he raised up slightly and looked over. Just below him a group of about thirty Indians was riding by. They were headed toward his camp! Buck was down there, and would be a prize for the Indians!

He couldn't beat them down there to rescue Buck. There really was nothing he could do but stay hidden, and wait. Now, he would be afoot out here, and a long ways from anywhere. Back to Big Timber would be the nearest.

Bart followed behind the Indian group, keeping out of sight. They were setting a fast pace, and he had to hurry to keep up. This was made all the more difficult, walking in his boots with his need to be quiet.

The Indians were getting near his campsite, and he knew any minute they would discover it. The Indians rode down to the water's edge and stopped. They dismounted and appeared to be preparing to camp for the night. They were within shouting distance of his camp!

Maybe he still had a chance. He waited until they had taken care of their horses, and were gathered around a small fire. Then he angled eastward to get around the group.

He could hear them laughing and talking as he eased his way through the trees and brush, taking care with every move that he didn't step on a branch or loosen a rock that would give him away.

He crawled across a large log that was in his way, and as he straightened up, he was looking into the eyes of an Indian, who had two feathers sticking up out of his head-band. Both men were shocked for a moment.

Bart dived for the man's middle, hitting him in the stomach with his head. The Indian grunted and they fell to the ground, each trying to get the first hold on the other.

From somewhere, the Indian produced a six-inch-long knife. He got loose from Bart's hold and jumped to his feet, then raised the knife and bent over, bringing the knife downward. Bart reached up and was able to grab the arm, then rolling over brought the arm downward, forcing the knife into the dirt.

Bart maintained enough pressure on the arm to keep the Indian from bringing the knife up out of the ground, but the man was able to keep hitting Bart on the head with his other hand.

Bart had to release his double handhold on the Indian's arm that was holding the knife, so that he had one hand to grab his own knife from the sheath on his belt. He didn't dare use his pistol; he'd have the whole Indian camp down on him.

When he got the knife out, he thrust it hard into the Indian's side, while still holding the Indian's knife arm with his other hand.

The Indian's knife arm relaxed, and then the man slumped over and was still. Bart held on until he was sure that the man was gone, and then let go and got to his feet. Sweat was pouring from him, and he felt weak.

He stood there a few minutes to get his breath back, and get his legs moving again. Then he hurriedly resumed his way around the Indian camp. If they discovered the dead Indian, his goose was cooked.

When he reached his camp, he could still hear the Indians talking and laughing. Any minute, one of them could wander over his way and discover him. He quickly and quietly put his gear back together, then saddled Buck, tied the gear behind the saddle, and led Buck quietly away from the Indian camp.

He led Buck for a quarter of a mile, keeping to the grassy areas where there wouldn't be a sound from the walking horse. When he thought he was far enough away, he climbed into the saddle and put Buck to a gallop to get as far away, and as quickly, as he could. He rode far into the night, until he thought that he and the tired horse could safely stop and rest for the balance of the night.

The little remaining oats in the sack didn't go far towards feeding Buck, but maybe he'd wait a little longer to start in the morning to give the horse a little time to graze. Bart rolled out his soogans and was soon fast asleep.

Crossing the Little Bighorn and Tongue Rivers, he made it into the village of Sheridan before nightfall.

He put Buck in a livery, arranged for his feed, and then found a hotel for himself for a room and a bath, and then went looking for some food.

A freighter pulled up in front of the cafe and two burly individuals came in and took a table. Bart walked over to them. "Say, did you fellows come up from the south?"

"Yeah."

"How are the roads down that way?"

"You've got good road all the way to Denver. When you get to Casper, you'll wanta go down the main road easterly along the Platte. There is a road that goes on south, but it runs out in the Laramie Mountains, and you don't wanta do that. The main road turns south again when it leaves the Platte River. Then it's a straight shot to Cheyenne and Denver."

"How long a trip is it to Denver?"

"If your horse can make forty miles a day, it'll take you about a week to Denver. There's even a bridge over the Platte."

"Thanks, I appreciate the information."

Bart had a meal of steak and eggs, followed by a piece of apple pie and coffee, then went back to his room for a good night's sleep.

The next morning, he was up before sunrise, grabbed some jerky, went after Buck and saddled him. Then reining the horse out into the street, he headed south.

Three days of uneventful travel found him pulling into Casper, where the next morning, he headed east along the Platte River.

He could tell that he was gaining elevation. The air was thinner, puddles were frozen over when he started out in the mornings, the sky seemed bluer, and the grass taller.

After another three days, he came down the long slope into Cheyenne, and another day crossing fertile cropland brought him into Denver.

Denver was a big city, by his standards. It took some time to locate a livery. He put Buck up and arranged for his feed, then found a room for himself. When the man handed him his key, Bart inquired about the trip to Dodge.

The man had a rough map that he brought out from his desk. Tracing one of the lines going east, he followed it with his finger. "This is the main road. When you get over here, you need to turn south. This road'll take you right in to Dodge City."

"How far is it to Dodge?"

"About a hundred and fifty miles."

Bart ran his finger along a line straight across country. "How far is it this way?"

"I don't know for sure. There are few roads that way, but I'd judge it to be around a hundred. You will have to ride around some farmed land once in a while that way."

Bart studied on it a while after he got up to his room. He finally decided to try the trip straight across country to Dodge.

The next morning he looked at the sun, judged which direction was southeast, and pointed Buck in that direction. The country was rolling with small hillocks, and shallow gullies that had to be crossed once in a while. There was lots of grass, and few obstructions. As the man had said, he did have a few farms he had to ride around, but Bart didn't feel that it slowed him very much.

He pushed Buck to what he believed to be about fifty miles the first day. It was a long day, and there was little daylight left when he finally stopped. He hobbled Buck and ate some hardtack and jerky before hitting the soogans.

Once again, he was up before daylight, had eaten some jerky and saddled Buck, then was on the way by the time the sun's rays hit the ground. That evening, awhile after dark, he and one tired horse pulled in to Dodge City.

He found a livery, got Buck taken care of, then found a room for himself. He located a restaurant and got a meal, and then seeing a saloon just down the block, went in for a beer.

He walked up to the bar and ordered his drink. When the bartender poured it and slid it down to him, he asked. "Do you know where I can find George Menton?"

"Sorry, never heard of him."

"He was the sheriff of Oklahoma City, and I heard that he might be in Dodge City, now."

"He hasn't been in here."

Bart paid for the beer, and found an empty table and sat nursing his drink, enjoying the good feeling of finally getting to his destination. It had been a long haul.

Bart walked slowly back to his room. He just felt really tired. It had been a long trip, and he had pushed it all the way. He was looking forward to a good, long night's sleep. He'd go looking for Menton tomorrow.

CHAPTER FIVE

The door slammed shut, and Slim came busting into the office.

"Al, thet bull's gotta go! I'm gonna shoot 'im, and hang his innards on a tree for the buzzards!" He strode around the room, first one way and then the other. He slammed his left fist into his right hand. "I jest cain't put up with 'im anymore!"

Al covered a smile with his hand. "What's the matter, Slim? Did he lick your belly button again?

Slim turned red. "No! I jest cain't do nothin' without him bein' right there mewlin' around, and stickin' his nose in everything I do! Those two slickers that you hired stand there snickerin', and makin' remarks. Thet knob-head jest hasta go!"

"Well, Slim, you know the boss has a special place in his heart for that animal. After all, you led him all the way from Texas, and the whole herd followed him. You might say he was the best trail hand we had. He just might fire the whole bunch of us if we let something happen to that bull."

"Wal, I cain't do my work with him pesterin' me. You gotta do somethin'."

"How are you coming with the holding pasture? You must about have it done?"

"The posts are set and all the wire strung but the west side. But every time I bend over to pick up a wire, or try to staple it, thet critter sticks his nose in where I'm tryin' to work, or butts my backside, wantin' me to pet 'im. He's gotta go!"

"Why don't you put him in the barn, tie him up, and you can feed and water him there until you get the pasture finished? It shouldn't take you more than a week to finish that pasture, and then you can leave him in there."

"I'll do 'er!"

Slim turned to go out the door, and Al laughed. "Or until you need your belly washed again."

Slim's face swelled up and turned red. "Gahwrrr- bah!" And he slammed the door, rattling the rafters, as he walked out.

Al walked into the cook shack and poured himself a cup of coffee, then sat at the table and watched as Carmelita finished washing the breakfast dishes and putting them away.

"Are you about ready to go to town? I was hoping to get away earlier, but we can order our supplies this afternoon, stay up there tonight, pick up the orders in the morning, and then come back."

"I be ready in half hour."

"All right, I'll go hitch up the team."

As they crossed the river and caught the road to Virginia City, Carmelita put her hand on Al's knee. "I glad we staying overnight. I love it out at the ranch, but is good to get away once in a while and do something different. Also, I eat somebody else's cooking."

"You've had a long straight spell of looking at the four walls there. It's about time you got away, all right. Hangin' around that ranch, you'll be gettin' old and fat and I'll need to find me a new woman."

"And I no longer feed you and you get skinny, and I throw you in the river for the fish to eat!"

They reached Alder Creek and started up the hill to Virginia City. Al could hear the placer mining over on the creek, and thought he heard something else. He looked around, and there were several riders coming up behind them. They were riding hard, and he got a bad feeling about them.

He whipped the team into a gallop. "Hang on. I think we had better make a run for it! He kept looking at the edge of town on the hillside above them, and then glancing around behind them. The riders were gaining on them. He whipped the team again with the reins. They were racing up the hill, the wagon swaying and swinging wildly with every bump or rock they hit in the road.

The riders pulled alongside them. They were a rough-looking bunch. One pulled in alongside Carmelita and rode, smiling leeringly at her. She edged over toward Al to get as far away from the man as she could. The man leaned over and put his hand on the side of the wagon, as if he were going to jump over onto the wagon. She reached down and pulled off a shoe and slammed it down on the hand. The man hollered and pulled back into his saddle.

Just then, one of the riders on Al's side pulled in next to the team and reached over to grab the horse's bridle. Al leaned over and got the whip out of its socket and slashed the man's outstretched hand. The man howled, and his hand went down toward the holster on his side. Al took one more swipe at the hand just as it was closing around the handle of the man's gun. Once more he howled, and fell back.

The riders all stayed right near the back of the wagon as Al kept the team running at full speed. They had to keep riding hard to keep up, but they stayed with the wagon, and Al was concerned that one of them would get up where he could jump into the back of the wagon, and he would have to deal with him then. He didn't want to shoot at them, because that might get them to shooting and could easily leave him shot and Carmelita at their mercy.

The riders were having a good time, shouting jeers and remarks as they rode alongside the wagon. They finally reached the outskirts of town and Al drove right down the main street, hoping that the riders would leave them when they got to town. It didn't work, however; they stayed right with them, yelling as they rode.

Al swung down the hill, the wagon rising up on two wheels as he did. The riders were forced to give a little, and fell in behind the wagon. Al drove full tilt down the hill, and swung into the lumber yard.

He pulled up next to the office and told Carmelita to jump out and run into the building. He stood up and faced the outlaws, his hand resting on the butt of his gun. He knew he didn't have a chance against the five gunmen, but he'd make a couple of them pay, anyhow.

The riders sat staring at him, their hands on the handles of their guns. The leader sat looking at Al. "Say, sodbuster, you whacked my hand with that whip o' yours. Nobody does that to me and lives. Draw your gun, or I'll fill you with lead where you stand."

Al was tempted to draw, but he knew that as soon as he moved, if the leader didn't beat him, one of the others would take it up. He didn't have a shot, whatever he did. He would just let the leader make the first move.

"No! The first one of you that moves'll be wearin' a buckshot jacket, and I've got another load for the next one that wants to die." Ike Barstow, the lumberman, stood on the porch with a greener, the hammer on both barrels clicked back.

The outlaws froze, staring at the shotgun barrels looking right at them. The leader suddenly wheeled his horse, and the rest followed him. Al watched them until they had reached the main street up the hill, then breathed a sigh of relief.

"Ike, you're the prettiest face I've seen in the last five minutes." He felt completely wasted, as if he had been dragged through a knothole. He climbed down off the wagon and followed Ike into the office.

Al sat down in a chair to regain his composure, while Ike found a couple of cups and poured Al and Carmelita a cup of coffee. "Here, drink this. How did you get that bunch stirred up?"

"They came up on us down on the road by the Gulch. We tried to outrun 'em, but they caught us before we reached the edge of town. I think you saved our lives, or at least, a damned miserable experience."

"Glad I was around. I sure hope that Bart has some luck getting that sheriff. This wild bunch is getting clear out of hand and we're goin' to have to do something about it. They's gettin' to be so many of 'em that they'll be takin' over the whole town, if somethin' ain't done."

Al and Carmelita repeated their thanks for running off the yahoos, said their goodbyes and drove up to the livery, put up the horses, and walked down to the hotel.

The next morning, after breakfast, they went around to the stores, getting their orders in for supplies. Carmelita held on to Al's arm as they walked. The streets seemed to be full of hard-eyed strangers.

When they had all of their orders in, Al took her back to the hotel, went up to the livery and hitched up the wagon, then, went around picking up all of the supplies. When the wagon was loaded, he returned to the livery and put the horses away again.

They slept until two A.M. in their room, then, they dressed. Al went for the wagon, picked Carmelita up, and they quietly left town.

Daylight was breaking as they crossed the bridge over the river and returned to the ranch. Al was steaming because they had to take such subterfuges to make what should have been a peaceful trip in to town for supplies. They just couldn't continue to live this way. We have to get rid of these galoots!

CHAPTER SIX

The morning was brisk when Bart left the hotel, but not nearly as cold as it had been in Denver the morning he left there! He stood on the porch, looking up and down the street. It was the usual scene of towns in this area. A central district with a cluster of brick, two-story office buildings, banks, and other business establishments, then beyond these, were the stores, saloons, barber shops, bawdy houses, and cafes, of various constructions. And beyond this, the dwellings.

Where in the world does he start looking for Menton? The businesses weren't open yet, so he decided on a café for breakfast and a slow cup of coffee, while he waited for the town to wake up.

After he had eaten and was on his second cup of coffee, the waitress came over to his table. "Would there be anything else?"

"No, but could you tell me, have you ever heard of George Menton?"

"No. Who is he?"

"He's a famous sheriff from Oklahoma City."

"I've never heard of him."

Bart finished his coffee, paid his bill, and returned to the street. There was a little more activity out there now. Several wagons passed by him as he stood there, and a few people were walking up and down the sidewalk. It still looked like a big town with a lot of places where a man of unknown description might be.

Well, he thought, maybe the logical place to start was the sheriff's office. Surely, the sheriff here would have heard of him. He thought he had seen the sign in front of one of the brick buildings down the street.

He walked down that way and when he looked closer, he could see bars in the windows of the building he had in mind. As he drew nearer, there was a sign over the door, 'SHERIFF'.

Bart walked in the door. A balding, slim man sat in the chair behind the desk. He looked up as Bart crossed the room. "Can I help you, young feller?"

Bart walked on over to the desk. "Yes, sir. I am looking for a man named George Menton. Do you know him?"

"I've heard of him. He was the sheriff down at Oklahoma City."

"I was told that he was here in Dodge."

"I would have known about it, if he was. What do you want him for?"

"Would he still be in Oklahoma City?"

"I wouldn't know. All I know is that he isn't here."

Bart's heart sank. Was he going to have to ride all the way to Oklahoma City, now? His backside was like tanned leather already, from pounding that kack. He turned to go. "Thanks, Sheriff." He walked out the door, onto the sidewalk.

As the door was closing on him, the Sheriff raised his hand. "Just a minute, young feller." But Bart had gone.

Bart went up to the livery. Maybe they would have seen the man.

The livery man was forking hay into some mangers when Bart came through the door. "Want your horse?"

"No. Just some information. Have you heard of a man by the name of George Menton?"

"No, I don't think so. Is he a rancher around here?"

"No, he was the sheriff down at Oklahoma City."

"Nope, never heard of 'im."

Bart spent the rest of the day going into saloons, cafés and stores, asking the same question, but with no better results. After he had eaten supper and gone to his room, he sat on the bed thinking of what to do next. It looked to him like the only thing left was to ride to Oklahoma City, and pick up the trail from there. That was going to add another couple of weeks to his trip, even if he found Menton right away.

Buck nickered as Bart came into the livery the next morning. "Yeah, you've been lying around eating oats and you're full of fire, aren't you. Well, this will probably take that out of you in a hurry. We've got some more country to see."

Bart rode out of the building and started to turn south, feeling discouraged about the long trek in front of him. He missed the ranch, missed Ruby, and wanted to be going the other way, toward home.

As he reached the outskirts of the city, he decided it might be an idea to have a letter of introduction from the sheriff here. He had said he knew of Menton. He turned Buck around and rode back to the sheriff's office and tied Buck to the hitch rail.

The sheriff was just pouring himself his second cup of coffee when Bart walked in. "Good morning. Would you like a cup of coffee?"

"Yes, thanks."

The sheriff poured two cups of coffee and handed one to Bart. "Have a chair, and what can I do for you today?"

"You said that you knew George Menton. I wonder if I could get a letter of introduction from you to the new sheriff down in Oklahoma City? I really need to find this Menton."

"What are you so interested in him for? Has he thrown you in jail sometime, or something?"

"No. I'm a rancher from up near Virginia City in Montana Territory. We are overrun by a bunch of outlaws, toughs, and other undesirables. It has gotten to the point regular citizens can't walk down the street and expect to get to the other end without being accosted. The city has asked me to find George Menton and see if I can talk him into coming up there to help us out. We hear he cleaned up Oklahoma City and other towns with situations like ours."

The sheriff sat studying Bart, as he sipped his coffee. The young man appeared honest, and straightforward. He seemed to be telling a plausible story. He guessed he'd take a chance.

"Young man, George will probably kill me for telling you, but I may be able to help you. George Menton is here. He retired when he left Oklahoma, told no one his name when he came here, and asked me to keep his secret. I doubt that he would go with you. He wanted to get away from the headaches of sheriffin'."

"Well, I've got to try. We need someone with his ability the worst kind of way."

"All right, take the street to the west here in front of the building. When you pass the "Big Bawdy", turn up that street to your right. The house on the right, next to the end one, is where George is at. He will probably shoot me for this, but you can give it a try."

Bart grinned. "Thanks, Sheriff. I owe you a lot. I wasn't looking forward to riding another hundred miles and maybe, even then, not finding him." He went out the door, whistling.

The house was a small, one-story building with a wide, covered porch in the front. It sat back a short way from the street in a lot with a picket fence around it. The house and the fence were in need of some paint.

Bart knocked on the door and it was opened by a man about six feet tall. He had laugh lines extending out from his eyes, a neatly-trimmed sandy mustache, a thatch of sandy hair, and a solid-looking, blocky build. "Good morning, young man. What can I do for you?"

"I'm sorry to bother you. I'm looking for a man named George Menton."

The man stood looking at Bart as if he were trying to figure out how to respond to the question. "Why do you want to see him?"

"Are you George Menton?"

Again the man stood, watching Bart, and finally said, "Yes."

"Mr. Menton, could I come in and talk to you?"

Almost reluctantly, the man stepped aside and indicated a chair for Bart and took one for himself in the small living room.

"Now then, how about telling me what's on your mind."

"Mr. Menton, my name is Bart Madison. I'm a rancher from Virginia City, Montana Territory. The city fathers have asked me to find you, rope you, and drag you to Virginia City. The town is overrun with outlaws, thugs, robbers and every kind of criminal. We are without any law enforcement, and our efforts to put a stop to their depradations have failed, and we need someone with your knowledge and ability to get rid of them."

"Son, I realize your predicament, and I sympathize with it, but I've quit sheriffing. I think you've made the long trip for nothing. I am retired. I have been a lawman so long that the badge is stuck to my chest."

"The council said that they would pay your old salary, if you would come."

"I left that salary to come here."

"Would you come if we doubled it?"

"Money doesn't mean that much to me. Not now."

"They will provide you with a house, meals, and even britches."

Menton sat watching Bart. Bart thought maybe he was making some progress. The man seemed to be considering it. Bart sat quietly watching him as he was mulling it over.

Bart started looking around the room while he waited for Menton to respond. There was a stove in one corner of the room, several chairs, and a gun rack hanging next to the window on his right. In one corner stood a fish pole and some outdoor clothing hanging on a hook.

"Mr Menton, I own a ranch that has a couple of miles of the best trout fishing in the world. The Ruby River is deep, green, and cold. You can't find better fishing than that. There is also a bunk there in the bunkhouse, and three squares a day, whenever you want to come fishing. I know there's not a better offer anywhere you would want to go."

Menton laughed. "Son, you should have been a politician! You have negotiating powers that many of them would love to have. Your council sent the right man! All right! You've won me over. I need a couple of days to set my affairs here in order. I'll meet you at the hotel day after tomorrow at sunrise." He stuck out his hand. Bart was surprised at the grip the older man had.

Bart retrieved his hat. "Thanks, Mr. Menton, there will be a lot of folks very happy that you've agreed to come. They are just flat out up against it right now."

He took his leave and returned to his room. He made his way at supper time up to the Burned Beef Café, where he had been getting his meals.

The waitress came over to take his order. "You look happy tonight. You must have had good news."

"I did, and tonight I'm goin' to celebrate. Bring me a choice steak, a cup of coffee, three eggs, and when I get done, a big piece of pie."

"I'll do that, and because it's such a grand occasion, I'll throw in some of cook's biscuits. She just took them out of the oven."

After he had eaten, Bart sat drinking his second cup of coffee. Had he really found the right man? After hearing of his exploits, he had pictured a man bigger than a barn, tough as nails, steely-eyed, with a swagger that took in both sides of a door. Instead, George Menton was of average size, he was soft-spoken, had a ready smile, twinkling eyes, and seemed friendly. He did have a solid build, like a brick wall, he would judge, and his grip was firm. Maybe he didn't get the right George Menton. Well, the sheriff knew him; he probably was. At any rate, he would be bringing a George Menton back - that's what he was sent to do.

CHAPTER SEVEN

The needle slipped, and when she jerked her hand back, it caught in the cloth and ripped out the last half-hour's sewing. "Damn! That hurt!"

Laughter erupted. "What did you say? Did I hear the epitome of cultural ladydom utter a blasphemous word?" Ginny giggled. "What would your handsome rancher say if he heard such language coming from the love of his life?"

"Just keep it up, and you can sew this dress of yours yourself. I stuck that needle in my thumb, and I think some blood got on the dress." Ruby handed the cloth to Ginny. "See, right there."

"Well, by the time you turn it under for the seam, no one could see it. Besides, this way I will take something of you to my wedding."

"I hope Bart will be back in time to go to it with me. He thought it might be a couple of months, and he wasn't sure just where this sheriff is. He has to find him before he can bring him back. He might be all winter!"

"He had better be back! Buster wants him to be his best man."

"Ginny, I just feel kind of lost. I don't know what I should do. I wish that I was in your shoes. Your man is right here, and will be here all the time. I see Bart maybe once a week, and then it is just for a few minutes while we go to the opera house, or somewhere to eat. Now, he's been gone for nearly a month, and I miss him."

"Well, ninny, you told him you wanted to wait. Just be glad he was willing to wait." She giggled. "Who knows? He might meet some good-looking dance hall girl down there in the south, and not even come back."

"If I could see him right now, I wouldn't wait! You're getting your wedding dress all ready, making plans for the house you're buying, and seeing Buster every night. I'm jealous!"

"If I were you, I'd be ready to go by the time he gets back, and rope him the minute he steps through the door. I don't think he would run very far."

"You may be right. I do love him very much. I just needed to get ready in my mind to leave home, and the store, and everything I have ever known. I'm ready, now."

"Good girl."

They spent the rest of the day working on Ginny's wedding dress. As she was leaving, Ruby gave Ginny a hug. "I'll see you tomorrow."

She left the house and started down the street. It was getting dark. The days were already getting shorter. She hurried along. One of the saloons was sitting along the boardwalk she had to take to get home. She hated to walk past it anymore. It was always full of ruffians, and it was even worse when it was dark.

She thought about crossing the street and walking down the other side, but decided she would just hurry past. Just as she reached the saloon door, a man staggered out and she had to stop to let him past her. He took a few steps across the walk and fell into the street. As Ruby started on again, two men walked out the door, bumping into her.

She could smell beer on their breaths, and she stepped back. One man grabbed her by the arm. "Jack, we have a lady amongst us. A pretty one, at that." He stood back, a leering grin on his face. He let go of her arm, and bowed. "I'm proud to meet you, Ma'am."

Ruby tried to walk around him, but he just kept sidestepping in front of her, staring boldly into her face.

"Get out of my way!"

"Oh, the lady wants to leave us. I'd say that wasn't even sociable, wouldn't you say, Jack?" He grabbed her arm again. "Now, why don't you just come in and have a drink with us, lady? We are friendly gents."

Ruby looked past the man. "Buster, shoot him!"

The men whirled around, and Ruby slipped past them and ran down the sidewalk. She ran all the way to the store, and slipped through the door without looking back. When she got inside and locked the door, she hurried upstairs and sat down in a chair in the living room, shaking.

Mabel Gray came rushing over and took her arm. "Ruby, what is the matter? You're pale as a ghost."

"One of those men in front of the saloon grabbed me on the way home. Oh, they are terrible! I hate them!'

Mabel put her arms around Ruby. "I know, darling. I hate them, too. I just wish that we could get rid of the whole bunch right now! The entire town is turned upside down since that bunch came in. We've got to do something. Your father has tried to organize the men, but none of them are lawmen, and there is no one that they are willing to follow to go after these brutes. I am getting so afraid. Our men are not gunmen. If they get into a battle, a lot of them will be killed. I hope that Bart is able to find that sheriff, and that he is willing to come. That's about our only hope."

"Mom, that's something I want to talk to you about. Bart asked me to marry him, and I've been reluctant to say anything because I know Daddy doesn't think a woman should live way out on a ranch. I've heard him say that women get out there and just wither away. I love Bart, and I want to marry him, but I've been afraid to mention it to Daddy. Could you kind of bring it up to him, and pave the way a little? I don't want him to be set against it when I talk to him about it. I know some families are split apart forever over things like that, and I would like to avoid that if I can."

"I like Bart. I think he is a fine young man. I know your father is pretty set in his ways, and feels that way about ranchers. I'll talk to him, and I'm sure it will be all right after he thinks about it a while."

"Thanks, Mom. I appreciate that."

CHAPTER EIGHT

Two days seemed like weeks. Bart got up late, walked to the café, ate breakfast, went back to his room, then went out again and walked around town. When he got tired of that, he walked up to the livery, borrowed a brush and brushed Buck until he was sure the hair was falling out.

When he tired of that, he put his saddle on the horse and rode out of town a ways. The endless prairie land, broken only by small brush-choked gullies, did little to catch his interest. After a couple of hours, he decided there was probably nothing but more of the same, so he turned Buck back toward town.

He was just itching to get home. He missed Ruby and the ranch more than he wanted to admit. She was in his thoughts most of the time. She was so beautiful, so smart, and so much fun to be with. He hoped that she would be safe until he got back. The waiting was almost more than he could stand.

He wondered what was happening at the ranch. They should be branding by now. He'd been gone almost a month. The hay should be up for winter. He was missing out on most of the fall work.

He hoped the new hands were working out. He should have been there to help get them started. Al was good with the working end of the ranch, but he wasn't much experienced at the business part of it. He hoped that was going all right.

He should never have made this trip. It seemed like someone else could have done it. Ruby had to make her way around town with the influx of the rough crowd to contend with. He just needed to get back with Menton, and start clearing out that bunch.

The sun was coming up over the horizon at about the fifth time Bart came back out of the hotel, where he had tied Buck to the hitch rail. He had his gear tied onto the horse, and time was a-wastin'. Where was Menton? He walked back into the dining room and poured himself another cup of coffee and sat down at the first table. He just wanted to get going!

About half way through the cup, Menton walked into the room. "Sorry I'm a little late. My new packhorse was a bit reluctant to take on the load. I'm ready when you are."

Bart set his half-empty cup and a coin on the table. "Let's go."

The sun was full-out when they rode out past the edge of town. Menton's packhorse was still resisting moving on, and pulled back on the lead-rope most of the time.

Bart watched the horse. "You say that's a new one?"

"Yeah, I bought him yesterday. He's young, and hasn't carried a pack before. He'll be pushing this horse by the time the sun goes down tonight."

The two men rode side by side, but little conversation passed between them. They stopped beside a small stream when the sun was high in the sky, let the horses drink and then hobbled them so they could graze for a short time, while the men had a meal of jerky and some biscuits that Bart had gotten from the cook that morning.

The ground was fairly level with only tiny depressions and small hills occasionally bringing some relief to the flat countryside they were riding through.

Time after time, they would ride by a piece of farmland plowed out of the existing grassland, with a sod shanty with a wisp of smoke coming out of a stovepipe. Most had chickens running around the yard, and some had a cow in some sort of corral. It looked to Bart like some hard-time living, for the most part.

That evening, as the sun was casting its last shadows, Bart pulled up at a level spot near a grove of oak trees.

"We'd better make it a day. Looks like there's enough wood here for a fire, and there's grass for the horses."

When they had the saddles off, and the horses hobbled, they rolled out their soogans, built a fire and had a meal of beans, potatoes, and the rest of the biscuits from the kitchen. Bart picked up the dishes and headed for the small stream running by, to clean them. "Sit back and rest. That was a long day's ride, and I imagine you haven't been on one of these for a while."

"You're right, there. My backside has been saying for several miles that it thought I had given up that kind of thing. There will be a couple of stiff legs in the mornin', too. I got to sayin' to myself: 'you really didn't have to agree to this'."

"Well, I and a lot of other folks are mighty glad that you did."

Denver was asleep when they rode into town late the next day. Bart rode up to the livery where he had stayed before, woke up the liveryman, and made arrangements to feed the horses. He also bought a sack of oats that they could carry on the packhorse to feed the horses when the grass was short.

The next morning, they found a café open, and had breakfast there before going on. The sun was out and, even in the high altitude, was fairly warm for the time of year. They rode into Cheyenne that night while there was still some daylight left.

After a night sleeping in the livery hay loft, Bart rolled out of his soogans, made his way to the outhouse behind the building, and as he returned, looked to the west. It looked like a cloud bank building up over the Rockies to the west. He shivered, remembering the storm he'd been in when he met Slim.

George was up and had his gear packed when Bart reentered the building. They got packed up, saddled the horses, and found a café where they bought a meal, then once again headed north. Bart kept looking to the west, watching the clouds build ever higher. It was colder than it had been, and it seemed to him that it kept getting colder as they progressed.

By noon, the clouds had moved over them, and the wind was picking up. The cold seemed to penetrate right through their heavy coats. They stopped long enough to get some jerky out of their saddlebags, and a drink of water, and then went on. It was too cold to just sit still and eat.

As the daylight was beginning to dim, Bart started looking for some kind of shelter to get out of the weather for the night. The wind was getting stronger all the time. He found a small cut-bank with a dry streambed, and they turned the horses into that. They unpacked and removed the saddles from the horses, then led them over to a stand of bushes growing along the bank. They tied the horses there, and fed them some oats.

While George was building a fire and getting their meal started, Bart walked up between the banks a ways and found a damp spot in a depression in the streambed. He got down on his hands and knees and dug out a hole in the gravel. A small trickle of water oozed into the hole.

Bart kept watching and, soon, enough water had seeped in for the horses to get a drink. He took them up one at a time and watered them. There would be water for them in the morning, as well. After that, he brought in more wood for the fire.

As they sat down to eat, the first snowflakes started to fall. George peered out into the darkness. "What is it doing, snowing already? Isn't this a month early for that?"

"This country is over a mile high. You can get snow about any time of the year, if conditions are right. Let's just hope that it's only a small storm passing through."

Bart made one more sashay back over to the brush patch and brought another armload of limbs so they could keep their fire going. "I don't like the looks of that storm. The wind is really beginning to howl. Why don't we take off that tarp you have your pack wrapped in and tie it to some bushes on the streambank. We can keep your gear under it and we can stay under, too, and keep out of the snow. I think we're goin' to get some."

They found some small bushes on the bank that they could tie the top of the tarp to, and some sticks they could use to hold the bottom of the tarp up on the other bank of the dry stream. There was room for Menton's pack and their saddles, and still some room for them to get underneath with their soogans. Their fire was close to the edge of the tarp and provided them with some warmth under there.

Sleep wouldn't come for Bart. He sat up and threw some more wood on the fire to keep it going. He could see snow gathering on the bottom of the streambed. That was going to make tougher going in the morning. Why couldn't it have held off for another week?

How many others had holed up in this wash to get out of a snow storm? The Indians that roamed these prairies before the white man came along, all of the trail herds that came north from Texas, Oklahoma, Kansas, wagon trains coming from the east, that were caught in one of these storms. There were a lot of tales that could be told if these hills could talk. Well, he knew of two that needed to put some miles behind them, or they might stay the winter. This was early for snow, even in this high country, but you never knew when an early winter could come along. He lay down again and tried to sleep.

The next morning, it was still snowing and there was nearly a foot of snow on the ground. George knocked the snow off the tarp, wrapped his gear back up, fed and watered the horses, then saddled them, while Bart put some breakfast together.

When they had eaten, they led the horses out of the stream bed, got mounted, and headed out. As soon as they were out of the protection of the wash, the snow began beating in their faces. It wasn't a heavy snow, and not piling up fast, but the hard wind sent the cold right through their clothing.

Both men pulled their collars up around their necks, tilted their sombreros down to keep the snow out of their faces, and let the horses have their heads.

By noon, the wind was even stronger. It felt to Bart that it was almost all he could do to stay in the saddle in the wind. He was leading the way, with George riding right behind him leading the packhorse. A grove of juniper jumped into Bart's vision, and he pulled his horse around to it. That cut off the wind, and he dismounted.

"What do you say to a fire? I think I lost my arms and both legs back there about forty miles."

George grimaced through the icicles hanging on his mustache. "I could do with a little heat myself!"

Bart scrounged around and found enough dry limbs under the trees for a fire, and soon had one going. They both hunkered around the fire until they finally got warm and dried off.

When they had eaten, George asked. "Are you going to go on this afternoon? I don't see this storm letting up very much."

"Yeah, I think we can make Casper by nightfall. I keep thinkin' that a nice warm bed and a good steak would sit pretty well."

"That is, if we make it. How do you know where you're going in this storm? You can't see fifty feet!"

"I have an advantage over you. I came this way about a week ago. I pick up a landmark every now and then, and we can just keep lookin' right into the wind. It's comin' off the north pole."

Mid-afternoon found them at the outskirts of Casper. They rode into the livery, and arranged for their horses, then made their way to the hotel, where they paid for a room.

Once they had dried off and warmed up, they walked up the street to a cafe for a meal. It was a small, one-story, sawed-lumber building. A sign above the door read, 'MAS'.

They found a table at the far end of the room near the fireplace and after they had seated themselves at the table, the heavy-set waitress came over. "What'll it be, boys?"

Bart said, "A big steak, well done, and smothered with eggs, and a hot cup of coffee."

"You have any pot roast, with mashed potatoes and gravy?" She nodded. "And some onions with it, if you have any."

When the waitress had returned to the kitchen, George said. "We haven't had a chance to talk much before. Tell me some more about this job."

"Virginia City is a small mining town. They made some rich strikes in what is called Alder Gulch. This is a small stream that runs right by the town. The town is situated on a hillside, with one main street that runs through the business district. There are several side streets, from the creek on one side to a small valley at the bottom of the hill on the other.

About five miles west of there is the Alder post office, then, in another two miles is the town of Nevada City. It is small, also, and this is where I understand a bunch of hard cases have come in and settled. Beyond that, is an outlaw hangout called Robber's Roost. All of this within ten miles of Virginia City. This rough bunch has been coming in to town and botherin' the townfolks, stopping women in the streets, threatening storekeepers, and so on."

"Have you had any trouble from that Robber's Roost place?"

"No, they even helped us with a problem we had before. Virginia City just went through the same kind of thing not long ago. People were afraid to leave their homes alone. A crooked sheriff was the head of that bunch, and they don't want something like that to happen again. That's why they sent for you. To get it stopped before it gets started again."

"Why me? It seems like you came a long way just to find a sheriff."

"Your reputation is way ahead of you. One of the councilmen had heard of the way you ran the outlaws out of Oklahoma City, and we decided that you are just what's needed to clean up our town."

"Will I be able to count on the townspeople to back me?"

"It took them a little while before to get them organized and go after the crooks, but they did, and they're willing now to do what's needed."

"Well, that's what it takes. The best sheriff in the world won't do much if the town's folks aren't behind him."

"What about you? Why did you finally decide to come? What is your history?"

"Not much to tell. I was raised in southern Texas, joined the Rangers when I got old enough and spent a few years with them. Then it was sheriffin' from one small town to another. Then folks started callin' me to fix trouble spots. Finally, they hired me in Oklahoma City. That was a tough one, and I decided when that was over to hang it up. I had enough to live on for a while and I could always find a deputy job somewhere, if things got slim again.

"I really wasn't all that anxious to take your job, but that fishin' river sounded pretty good, and if I could get a job that paid enough to keep food on the table and there was some good fishin', that sounded like a winning hand to me. How did you get involved in all of this? You said your ranch was ten miles, or something like that, from town."

"My partner and I rounded up a herd of wild cattle in Texas and herded 'em up to Montana. We found some land on the Ruby River and put together a ranch there. Maybe I should say we're putting together a ranch there. The woman I'm going to marry lives in Virginia City, and her parents own a store there. Her father is one of the city councilmen, and they are the ones that asked me to make this trip."

The waitress came over to their table with a large platter filled with steak and eggs and a plate of pot roast covered with onions, and mashed potatoes swimming in gravy, and the two fell to eating.

After they had eaten and Bart paid for the meals, he suggested that they take a turn around the town. The bad weather had abated and a glimmer of sunshine was trying to find a way through the clouds. After they had covered most of the town, walking down one side of the main street and back the other, George stopped in front of the Golden Nugget saloon. "What say we have a beer before we turn in for the night? This time, I'll buy. You've paid for everything so far this trip."

"The council gave me money for the trip. That's what it's for."

Bart bought two beers and they went back to a table against one side wall. After he was seated, he looked around the room. There was the bar all the way across the back of the room. It was inlaid with silver dollars across the top. A large mirror was behind the walkway in back of the bar, and shelves of liquor stood below the mirror. A piano stood against the wall to their right, and the rest of the room was filled with tables.

George raised his bottle. "Here's to a safe trip."

"I'll go with that, but we've a lot of miles to go, yet."

They sat for some time enjoying their beer, watching the customers talking and playing cards, and soaking in the heat of the room.

Presently, three rough-looking men got up and walked over to their table. The one in the middle led the way. He stood in front of George.

"Mister, aren't you George Menton?"

"I might be, why?"

"You shot my brother"

George didn't change expression. "Oh, who was your brother?"

"Chuck Flannery. You shot him in cold blood."

George maintained his friendly expression. "I don't recall the name, but if I shot him, it was called for."

"You shot him in cold blood, and you're gonna pay for it."

"Where did this happen?"

"In the Gold Nugget saloon in Oklahoma City"

"I seem to remember a shooting in that place. Your brother was a tall, slim cowboy? He was pushing it, just as you are, and drew on me. I didn't have a choice. Now, the best thing for you to do is pack it in, and go have a beer."

"Menton, you are supposed to be such a hot-shot sheriff, and you may be fast with a gun, but there are three of us, and both of my pards are fast as I am. One of us is goin' to beat you. You're as good as dead!"

Bart glanced at George. His demeanor hadn't changed that much, but his eyes were pure cold steel. George pointed at the talker's belly. "If you move one muscle, that button right above your belt buckle is going to be a button-hole. Now, as to your friends there, my partner is faster than I am, and between the two of us, they won't be in any better shape."

George continued to stare into the man's eyes, while Bart moved his hand to the grip of his pistol.

The entire room was silent; everyone there was looking at the scene going on at Bart's table. Flannery's muscles twitched. Bart could tell that he wanted the worst way to pull his gun. The man's two companions stood with their hands hovering over their weapons. Any minute, the whole place could erupt into gunfire.

The talker stared at George until he finally had to drop his eyes. He muttered, "All right, you've won this round, but I'll get you sooner or later." He turned and left the building, followed by his companions.

Bart let out a gust of air. "Whew, that was a narrow one! I thought that both of us were going to bite the dust."

"You never know. Nine times out of ten, they will back down, especially if they've been drinkin', but it's that tenth one that'll get you. Well, drink up. I'm ready for that soft bed you were talkin' about."

Bart lay thinking about the day's travel, and of the scene in the saloon. He had to smile. George might seem mild, and easy-going, but when the chips were down, he was like a brick wall. The council had picked the right man, all right!

The horses were saddled the next morning, and Bart was helping George get ready to load his pack on the packhorse.

"George, do you have room for a full sack of oats? We'll be going cross-country from here on for a while. After a couple of days, we'll be in desert, and there's little feed there. We'd better pack something for the horses."

"We can do it."

Bart went into the tack room to pay the livery man, and purchase the sack of oats. The sun was just peeking over the horizon as the two left the city limits. The weather favored them, and as they left the higher country, the snow cover grew thinner, until it finally disappeared altogether.

As Bart had predicted, after a couple of days, the vegetation became scarce, and soon it was cactus and Indian grass, with some salt cedar in the draws and an occasional juniper, for vegetative cover.

On the fourth day, when they stopped for lunch, George looked around. "There isn't even enough around here to eat for a rattlesnake, or a horned toad!"

"No, they just go into hibernation, and wait until some tired old sheriff comes along, and they feast on him."

"Well, if you don't quit pounding this old sheriff's backside in that saddle, there won't be anything for the rattlesnake there, either."

"We're in Montana Territory, now. We'll camp on the Shoshone River tonight, and from there on, there'll be more feed. These mountains to our right are the Bighorns. We're goin' to have to keep our eyes peeled for a couple of days. It's Crow country to our right for that long, and Absaroka to our left. We might be in Absaroka country a day longer. At least, from now on there'll be feed for the horses.

"Tomorrow, we'll be going near the place where Custer made his big mistake."

"Well, I hope that we don't make the same one."

"Yeah, the Crow are pretty fierce. After tomorrow, we'll be across the Yellowstone, and from what I hear, the Crow don't usually travel on that side of the river. It's pretty much Absaroka country, and they are a little more friendly."

They made the crossing of the Shoshone River without incident, but when they came to the Yellowstone, the river was higher than it had been when he came through weeks before. Bart rode up and down a ways to try to find a crossing, and finally decided that they would have to swim it.

He led off, and George waited on the bank with his horse and the packhorse until they could see if a crossing was possible, and where the best place was to attempt it. Bart found an area where there was footing for the horse most of the way with only a short distance that was too deep for the horse to get footing. He pointed it out to George and he followed that path across the river.

They made camp on the other side, built a fire, and dried out. After they had eaten, and had the horses staked out for the night, Bart said, "We'd better let that fire go out. We just don't need to invite some Absaroka's in for supper."

In the middle of the night, Bart woke up and looked around. He couldn't see anything, nor hear anything, but something had stirred his senses. He had a feeling that someone was watching him. He pulled on his boots and walked away from the still-glowing coals, to try to get his eyes adjusted better to the darkness.

Suddenly, he was staring into the face of an Indian, and just then, two more stepped in front of him. The first one had a spear not a foot from his stomach, and the Indian was waiting for him to make a hostile move. The Indian motioned for him to move back to the fire. When they arrived there, Bart could see five or six more, standing with spears poised over the sleeping George. He knew that one false move by either of them would be the end of both of them.

He said quietly, "George, we have visitors. Sit up slowly. They have spears looking at your belly button."

George sat up. "What's going on?"

"We have some Indian friends came to visit. Just move slow, and I'll try to talk to them. I think they're Absarokas. At least, I hope so."

Bart looked over to the Indian that he had picked out as the leader, and pointed to George, and then to himself. "We friends, we come in peace."

The Indian motioned for them to saddle their horses, and had four Indians guard them. While this was going on, the rest of the Indians were going through the pack and scattering everything around on the ground. They picked up anything they might want, but most things didn't interest them much.

When the horses were saddled, the Indian motioned for Bart and George to mount up. They were relieved of their weapons and forced to ride off, surrounded by what Bart estimated to be about fifteen young Indians.

George was riding by his side with two Indians on one side and two on the other, and the rest following them. George said, "Looks like we got ourselves a pickle here. How're we goin' to get out of this one?"

Bart remembered this had happened to him once before when he was driving the cattle north. That time, he had cattle to trade for his release. He didn't have anything this time.

"Just be thankful it wasn't the Crows that caught us. We'd probably be staked to an anthill by this time. I don't see anything to do right now but go along with them and hope for the best."

After several hours, they came into a small meadow, fairly high into the mountains. The meadow was filled with teepees, and older men, women, and young children were milling about. The lead Indian motioned for them to dismount, and when they were on the ground, they were tied to a small tree near the compound.

Bart tried to talk to several of the Indians that walked by them, but no one seemed to understand English. He tried to loosen his bonds, but they were tied tight, and all he accomplished was grinding the ties into his arms, and there was no way he could use sign language with his arms tied.

Toward evening, a young Indian woman brought bowls of food over. She came up to Bart first and held the bowl up to his lips. He swallowed the food as she tilted it into his mouth. When he finished the bowl, she set it down and smiled at him. She was the one that had fed him when he was here the first time! He tried to talk to her, but she just smiled at him, and then went over to feed George. When George had eaten, she left them.

Would she help them? How could he communicate with her? That evening, as the sun was going down, the Indians built up a community fire, and for a time, there was much singing and dancing around the fire. No one paid any attention to the two prisoners. Sometime after dark, the Indians all retired to their teepees, and it became quiet.

Once again, while they were alone, Bart worked at his ties. He rubbed them up and down against the bark of the tree hoping it could wear the leather through, but the bark rubbed his wrists raw, and the leather held. He looked over to the tree where George was tied, and in the dim light from the dying fire, it looked like George was doing the same.

The next morning, once again, the same Indian woman brought their food. Bart tried to show her his bonds, and to ask her to turn him loose. Again, all he got for his efforts was a smile. His bones ached from standing against the tree, and it was all he could do to remain erect. George indicated he was in the same condition. How could they get out of this?

The same Indians that had captured them left on another foray. Bart had a slight hope that maybe, with the warriors gone, the young woman would come by and loosen his bonds. Toward evening, she came once again, fed them, and left. There was no way he could communicate with her. He tried smiling at her, and she smiled back, but then went on about her duties.

Night came again. He was getting weak from standing so long. He was tied to where he couldn't slide down to sit, and leaning back against the tree was the only way he could relieve the pressure on his legs. He felt like leaning out against his bonds and just hanging there.

The first indications of the coming dawn were just beginning to provide a little light. Bart tried to adjust his bonds to relieve some of the pressure on his wrists. He felt something on his left arm, and tried to look over his shoulder to see what it was. The Indian woman was standing there with a knife in her hand. She quickly severed his ties, handed the knife to Bart, and stood smiling.

Bart nearly fell on his face when his bonds were released. When he could stand, he walked over and cut George loose. George started to fall, and Bart caught him. When George could stand, the Indian woman indicated to them to be quiet, and led them through the camp. Bart was sure that they would step on an unseen branch, or something that would wake the encampment.

They walked so close to some of the teepees that he could reach out and touch them. As they slipped past the last teepee, Bart could hear some talking inside. His heart jumped. They couldn't get caught now. They were almost free! They continued on a short way, then, the woman stopped and pointed into a grove of trees. Their horses were tied there!

Bart grabbed the woman and hugged her. She looked up and smiled at him, then motioned for them to go. It didn't take any persuading on their part. They soon were on their way! It felt good to get their horses under them, and travelling again.

As soon as it was light enough to see, Bart put their horses into a lope. He turned the horses into the trail that the Indians had brought them in on and headed back toward their camp. He was as anxious as he could be to put as much distance between them and the Indians as he could. George was right behind him. Whew! What a relief!

After a couple of hours, Bart was starting to feel good. They should have put enough distance between them and the encampment that they could slow down. Both horses were tiring, and blowing. He slowed to a walk.

Coming to a small stream, Bart stopped. They got off their horses and let them drink from the cool water. Bart got down on his belly on the stream bank and drank his fill, with George following suit.

He was looking into the stream, getting ready for one more drink before going on, and saw the reflection of an Indian standing there across the water from him.

How did that happen? How could they have caught them? They had pushed their horses as fast as they could, and the Indians, when they discovered they were gone, would have had to catch their horses and follow them. It just couldn't be!

He stood. There were Indians all around them. More than before. Just when it seemed they had made their escape, here they were again! The only good thing he could think of was that the Indians hadn't killed them right at the start.

George said, "It looks like we're in a whole pickle jar now, and we don't even have our guns."

Bart gestured to the Indians, "We are friends. We are friends." As before, no one understood him. He pointed to his heart, and then to the heart of the nearest Indian. "Friend."

The Indian he had pointed to whirled around and disappeared back into the trees. What was that all about?

George looked over at Bart. "What happens now? Are we going back and hold that tree up again?"

"I don't know. This looks like a war party, or maybe a hunting expedition. These are older men, and better armed. I don't like the looks of it. They might do away with us right here. One good thing is that they are Absarokas. That might mean something."

They waited with several Indians standing around them, their spears at the ready.

George looked up. "Oh-oh, here comes the chief. We'll find out really soon. I can feel that spear going in my back right now!"

The Indian chief walked over to where the two were standing. When Bart could see his face, he got a grin a mile wide. "White Eagle! It's me, Bart."

The Indian looked more closely at Bart, then, got a smile on his face. He walked over and grasped Bart by both arms. "My brother! Good to see you."

"How is your father?"

"He is well. You bring cow?"

"Not this time. My village has trouble." He pointed to George. "This is George. He came to help my people."

The chief looked at George. "You brother to my brother, you brother to me." He turned back to Bart. "Go with the wind, brother." Then he smiled. "Next time, bring cow." He stood back and waved them on.

They mounted their horses, and waving to the chief, went on down the trail. Bart kept up a fast pace until they reached their previous camp. There was nothing left of any value to them. The Indians had pretty well cleaned it up.

George looked curiously at Bart. "How is it that you happened to know that Indian Chief out here in the middle of nowhere?"

"We were captured right there when we were headed for Montana the first time. We promised White Eagle cattle when we came north again with the herd, and they let us go. When we came through again, we kept our promise."

As they were getting ready to go on, George said, "You live an exciting life around here. Have you got any more surprises for me as we go along?"

'No. Tonight we'll be in Big Timber. I'll get some more blankets and some food there. We should be out of Indian country from there on. The Gros Ventres and the Assiniboines and the Blackfeet are all further north."

It was well after dark when they rode into the village of Big Timber. Bart reined his horse in at the livery. When the horses were taken care of, he led the way to the hotel, where he arranged for a room. They ate in the dining room of the hotel, and then went to bed. It seemed like pure luxury to Bart. No rocks under his bed, and no pine needles falling into it.

The next two days found them riding down the main road along the Yellowstone River. The road was filled with travelers of every description. Some were on horseback, some in buggies, and some in wagons laden with materials of every kind.

On the evening of the second day, they rode into the town of Bozeman, nestled in a bend of the river. Once again, they took their horses to the livery and then found a hotel room. The loss of their packhorse to the Indians had made camping out a little frugal. Jerky and hardtack didn't stretch as far. Bart led the way to the café where he had eaten on the way out.

They found a table and the waitress came over for their order. She smiled. "Would you like a swim before I take your order?"

Bart turned red. He looked at George, not knowing what to say, then, back at the waitress. "I—uh—I—uh, just a steak and eggs, please."

George said, "Would you have a pot roast with spuds and onions? I'd like some of that." When the waitress left, he said, "As I said, you live an interesting life around here. What was that about?"

Bart turned red again. "Nothin'."

"It didn't sound like nothin'."

"There's a hot springs across the river. I took a swim in it, and she and another girl saw me there. That's all."

"Like I say, you lead an interesting life around here. I think I might stay and see how you northern people live. How much further is it?"

"Two days."

"Two days, that's good. I was beginning to think that we were going to come to the edge of the world one of these days. My rump has grown ripples."

The lights were showing down below them as they topped the ridge. The road was wide, and Buck knew the way. Bart knew it was late, but he wanted to finish the trip. He was bone-tired and wanted to get it done.

They rode to the livery first and took care of the two horses. Then they walked toward the haberdashery. He knew James Gray would have closed by now, but he also knew that he would be glad to know that the trip had been successful.

CHAPTER NINE

This was the fourth day of the rain; heck, it wasn't rain, it was a creek turned upside down and coming out of the sky. Mud was a foot deep everywhere, creeks were running rampant, and little draws were formed, coming off the hill. It looked to Al as if the whole country was going to wash away. He wished that Bart would get back. He could get back to working the cattle, and Bart could have the headaches of running the ranch. Where in heck was he? He should be back by now.

Shorty had just gone up to the barn to get some rope. The Ruby was running high, and he had said it was up to the bridge. That's all they would need—to have the bridge wash out. He went to the barn to help Shorty find some rope.

"Did you find the rope, Shorty?"

"I found one, but we need about three."

"What do you need so many for?"

"There's a big log that came down the river and it's jammed against the bridge. The water's caught it and it might buckle the bridge. We're gonna get a rope around it and pull it out of the water."

"There's some lariats hanging on the wall in the tack shed. Take them. I'll pick up a couple things and be down and give you a hand."

Shorty got the ropes and rode back down the hill to the river.

Al returned to the house, retrieved his slicker, and told Carmelita he would be down at the river with the boys. He saddled his horse and started down the hill. He could see the large log bucking at the bridge from the force of the water. Surges of water were spilling over the log, and geysers of water were splashing high above the men on the bridge. Limbs and debris of every sort were thrown up onto the bridge, making it slippery for the men trying to keep their feet on the muddy surface.

Al ground-reined his horse, and just as he stepped up onto the bridge, a surge of water knocked him off of his feet, and washed him across the structure. He realized he was going over the bridge and into the rushing water beyond. As his body washed over the bridge, he was able to get a small hold on the plank nailed across the end of the bridge boards. He held on for dear life, but could feel that his hands were slipping on the wet wood.

Slim looked over just in time to see Al go. "Shorty! There!" He pointed to Al as he ran to help. The two men quickly knelt by Al and each grabbed an arm. They braced a foot against the plank and desperately tried to pull Al back against the raging current. Slowly, Al was coming back up over the edge of the bridge.

Just as they had the top half of his torso lying on the bridge, a huge wave came up over the upstream side, and crashed over them. Shorty lost his hold on Al, and the crush of the water washed him back to one side, with only Slim's hold keeping Al from going back into the water. Strong as he was, Slim could feel Al slipping out of his grip.

Shorty rushed over and grabbed Slim's arm, and then reached further down and was able to get hold of Al's arm, as well. Still the raging water was so strong that both of them could not pull Al up.

Suddenly, the bridge was pushed upward by a surge of water. Slim was sure they were going downstream, but the structure settled back on its pinnings. As it was up in the air, it released the water pressure on Al, and they were able to pull him up onto the bridge. They laid him flat on the deck.

Slim sat, trying to get his breath back. "Shorty, kin you imagine a guy wantin' to go fer a swim when they's all this work to be done?"

Al sat up. "Thanks, guys. I'd've been a goner if you hadn't grabbed me. I could feel my hands slipping off that plank." He looked over to where the log was bouncing on the upstream side of the structure. "That log is causing all the problem, isn't it." He could see the bridge itself rise perceptibly, and then settle back on its underpinnings. The force of the raging water against the log was going to force the bridge from its foundation if they didn't get it out of there quickly.

Slim nodded. "We got to git thet buster loose or the bridge is goin'. Shorty, let's get back on them ropes. We gotta git a choke-hold on that thing and pull it out, or its goodbye Grandma fer thet bridge."

Al got up and went to the west end of the bridge to check the underpinnings. Were they going to hold? Both of them on that end were still intact, but there was considerable give and they could tear loose at any time. If they did that, the bridge was downstream.

When he looked up again, Slim was snaking himself off of the bridge and onto the end of the log to try to get a wrap on one end with his lariat. By the time Al got across the bridge, Slim was entirely on the log and attempting to get a loop in the rope over the end of the log. The force of the water kept pushing the rope away from the large timber.

The log was bouncing against the bridge so hard that it was difficult for Slim to hang on. He had his legs around the log as if riding a horse, and was leaning over the end of the log trying to get the rope around it.

Al looked around to see if he could see a limb or something he could use to push the loop down under the surface and back around the bottom of the log. He saw one just past the end of the bridge and started for it. The top end of the log was in the water over in the same direction. He started for the limb, and suddenly the end of the log Slim was on was sucked under the bridge. The end near Al rose high in the air and then splashed down in the water, raising a column of water as high as a tree, and the entire log was sucked under the bridge.

Water that the log had held back surged under the bridge and the log ground gratingly along the underside of the bridge as the water forced it through. When the log surfaced on the far side of the bridge, the water pressure forced the log to bounce clear out of the water, and then it settled back and was carried on downstream.

Al and Shorty rushed over to the downstream side of the bridge, looking for some sight of Slim. He was nowhere to be seen. Al ran back to where he had ground-reined his horse, jumped into the saddle, and galloped down along the river, trying to get a glimpse of Slim.

He finally caught up with the log, and scanned the river all around it for some sign of Slim. He should have been carried down the river about the same speed as the log. He was nowhere to be seen. He decided to keep pace with the log, and Slim should show up somewhere along the way.

Al had to go around a clump of trees, and when he got back to the river, he looked until he found the log again. He looked around the water that was near the log; there still was no sign of Slim. Just as he looked back toward the log, Slim's head appeared just above the racing timber. One arm came up holding on to a limb as the log rolled sideways, and Slim pulled himself back onto the log.

Slim sat up on the log as if he were riding a horse, whipping the bark as he rode. He saw Al, and waved. Then Al started laughing, as much from relief as anything else. Slim was singing, "*There never was a cowboy who hadn't been throwed—There never was a log that hadn't been rode.*" Well, that happy-go-lucky cowboy was all right!

Al rode on ahead, and found a bend in the river that would force the log in near the shore. He waited until the log came in toward him and was able to toss his rope to Slim. Slim grabbed the rope, slid off the log, and Al pulled him ashore.

"Slim, that was a damned fool thing to do! I thought sure you were a goner. How did you get back on that log?"

"Shucks, Boss. It was jest like brandin' a steer. I jest grabbed its tail, and hung on. The worst was its tail stayed under the surface and I swallered enough water t' fill a jug."

"Well, let's get you back to the house and dried off. Climb up."

As they crossed back across the bridge, Al stopped the horse and looked at the water. It was flowing smoothly under the bridge, now that the log was out of there. It would be fine now, unless there was more rain and the river rose some more. They picked up a relieved Shorty and the horses and went on back to the house.

As they walked in the door, Carmelita took a look at Slim. "Senor Slim! Dios mio! Que pasa? Are you all right?"

"Yep, I'm fitter'n a fiddle on Saturday night."

"I see the cuts. You peel off that shirt. I fix!"

She went into the other room and soon returned with a pan of hot water, some salve, and some cloth to bind his wounds. When she had finished, she said. "There, Senor Slim. Now, you better."

"Thanks, Carmelita. You're gooder'n a plate o' hotcakes when your belly's hollerin'!"

She laughed. "You go lay down, get some rest, and I fill that hollow belly."

The doorbell jingled as the door swung open. Ruby reached down to the shelf under the counter for the gun that her father had purchased. She hated that. It used to be so calm. You looked forward to seeing your friends and neighbors when the door opened; now, you were afraid every time that it would be one of those outlaws coming in. Even if they were actually going to buy something, they looked at you, and your skin crawled.

She breathed a sigh of relief. It was Ginny!

"Hi, Ruby." She laughed. "Are you going to shoot me?"

"Oh, Gin! I'm so tired of all of this. Those thugs running all over town all the time! You get so you're afraid to walk out of the door. I wish that Bart would get back! I hope he could find that sheriff. Dad said that he was a good one, and had cleaned up Oklahoma City."

"Me, too. Two of the bad ones even came into Buster's shop wanting him to shoe a horse for them. He was busy with a job and told them to come in the next day. They came at him right in the shop. Buster picked up a hammer and told them to come ahead, and they backed off and left. It's getting really scary."

"Have you set the date, yet?"

"Yes, New Year's Day. I wanted it sooner, but Buster wanted to get his house fixed up first."

"What is he doing to it?"

"He already put a new stove in the kitchen, a new sink, and some cupboards. Now, he is putting new windows in the living room, and he is putting a new interior wall in there. He also ordered a large wool rug for that room."

"What about the bedroom? Isn't he fixing that, as well?"

"He redid that earlier."

Ruby giggled. "Of course; how silly of me."

"Ruby! Buster says that if it keeps on like this, he's going to try to get the vigilantes going again. They did a lot in getting that old sheriff out of here."

"Do you remember how they had us tied up in the basement of the courthouse? I was so scared."

"Me, too. Why do we have to have so many mean people in the world? Why can't everybody be nice?"

"My dad says that this sheriff has cleaned up a lot of towns in the south, and gotten rid of the riffraff there. I hope that Bart can find him and get him to come here. I don't see how one man can get all of these skunks out, though."

"Maybe he's as big as a barn and tough as nails, or something."

"He'd have to be. Come on upstairs and I'll put on some coffee."

CHAPTER TEN

The store windows were dark when Bart and George walked up the steps of the haberdashery. There was a light in the upstairs window. Bart knocked on the door, and shortly, the store lights came on and the door opened. Jim Gray stood in the opening. "Bart! Oh, it's good to see you, boy! Come in, come in."

Bart and George entered the room. Bart reached over and touched George's arm. "Jim, this is Geo—"

"Bart! Oh, Bart! You're back!" Ruby came rushing down the stairs, threw her arms around his neck, and hugged him until he thought he would fall over. "Oh, I'm so glad!"

George got a grin on his face. "Does some woman come give you a hug every time we stop?"

She let go of Bart and stepped back, looking up into his face. "What does he mean - some woman hugged you every time you stopped?"

George kept a straight face, "Oh, let's see. Denver was that pretty little Mexican girl. Cheyenne was that blond woman; Casper, as I remember, was that cute little brunette with the dimples. Then, there was the little Absaroka up in the mountains, the older woman in Big Timber, and the redhead in Bozeman. I think that was all. Maybe there were two women in Denver. I can't remember, for sure."

Ruby said to Bart, "What does he mean, all these women hugged you? What have you been doing all this time?"

Bart looked daggers at George. "There may be more than outlaws after your hide. I think you'd better 'fess up!"

George laughed. "I'm sorry, Ma'am, I couldn't help it. This man has had outlaws shootin' at me, drug me through the dangdest blizzard you ever saw, got me captured by Indians, and took me away from my comfortable home, just to come up here and get shot at some more. I had to get even with him, somehow. He has been a perfect angel."

"Well, he better have." She hugged Bart once more.

Bart said, "Well, as I was saying, this is George Menton, and, George, meet Jim Gray. This tornado here is his daughter, Ruby."

Jim Gray stuck out his hand. "Mr. Menton, I can't tell you how glad we are to see you. We have a real mess here, and badly need someone with your abilities to straighten it out."

"Bart filled me in on your problem. I don't know if I can solve it or not, but I'll give it my best shot."

"We couldn't ask for more. I'll call a meeting in the morning with the others and you can meet them."

Bart said, "Why don't I take George over to the hotel and get him settled in. I'll come back for a little while, Ruby, but we're about tuckered out."

They all said good night, and Bart led the way to the hotel, arranged for their rooms, and went with George up to his. "I'll come by about eight and pick you up, and we'll go find some breakfast."

"Sounds good. Don't stay up too long with that little gal of yours. Good night."

"Night, George. Have pleasant nightmares." He grinned, and left for the haberdashery.

Ruby was sitting behind the counter when Bart walked in. She jumped up, ran over to him and threw her arms around his neck. "Oh, Bart, I've been so lonesome for you!" She stood on tiptoes and kissed him.

"I've missed you too, Ruby. Every time I got delayed, I just itched to get going again." He brought her face up again and kissed her long and hard. "Next time your Dad has one of these trips in mind, I'll tell him to send Buster." He laughed. "He can take his hammer to the Indians."

"Are you going back to the ranch tonight?"

"I told George I would take him to breakfast tomorrow, and, then, after the meeting, I'd take him around to get acquainted with the town, and I'll probably take him down as far as Robber's Roost, so he'll know about it. Then, I'd better drop off at the ranch on the way back and see what's happening there. He can find his own way back here."

"I wish you would come back here, too."

"I just have to get back to the ranch. Al has had to do the whole thing for a couple of months now. Hard to tell what all has happened since I left. I'll try to get back in a couple of days, if I can."

"You'd better. I want you to know I've changed my mind. We can get married tomorrow, if you want. I don't want to be away from you that long again."

"Ruby! That's great! You've just made me the happiest man in the world." He picked her up and danced her around the floor. "By golly, that trip was worthwhile, after all!"

"All right, go now. I can tell you're tired. Just get back up here and see me. We can talk about it, then."

"Yeah, my tail is kinda draggin'. I'll be back in a couple of days. I love you."

"I love you, too. Now go to bed."

The sun was peeking over the horizon, and streaming through the window when Bart left his room and went to wake George. George was up, and opened the door to Bart's knock.

Bart walked into the room. "Ready to go?"

"Yep."

Bart led the way to the café, and they entered. They found an empty table near the wall, and took it. When the waitress came over, she looked at Bart.

"Aren't you the one who went after that sheriff?"

"Yes."

"Did you find him?"

"This is the man. Meet George Menton, the new sheriff of Virginia City, and hereabouts."

"Mister, your breakfast's free this morning. You don't know how much people have been waiting for you. My name's Flora. What'll you have?"

"Bacon, eggs, and pancakes."

She turned to Bart, "And you?"

"Same."

She returned to the kitchen. George said, "Well, this day is starting out pretty good."

"Well, the day ain't over. After we meet with the council, I'll give you a whirlwind tour of the country around here so you'll be familiar with it."

"Yeah, that would be a big help. Sometimes you have to know where the road to retreat is, or which way the outlaw may be coming from."

The merchants were seated in the Gray living room when Bart and George arrived. Jim Gray ushered them into the room and introduced George to the group.

"All right, we all know why we're here. Sheriff Menton, this town is overrun with outlaws, toughs, thugs and every other nondescript person you can imagine. It is so bad our womenfolk can't safely go out on the street. We had a crooked sheriff a couple of years ago, and we were able to get rid of him, but we haven't been able to replace him since then.

"We are just finishing the jail. Buster Kilgore, there, is putting the bars and steel cells in. He's our local blacksmith. When will it be finished, Buster?"

"I should have it done in a week, or thereabouts. I would appreciate you coming over, Sheriff, and taking a look. You might have some ideas about how it's done, that I don't. I've never made a jail before."

Jim continued. "This is Ike Barstow. He's building your house. It's right next to the jail. That should make it handy for you. The courthouse is just across the street from it. We told Bart to tell you we would match your last salary, furnish a house, and pay your expenses, board and room. We had planned on seventy dollars a month salary. Is that satisfactory?"

George studied a minute. Everyone thought he was searching for the words to ask for more money.

"That'll do fine."

Jim continued. "This is the group you can count on. There are others in town that may help, but this is the core group."

"Are there any former law officers among you?"

No one answered. Jim said, "We all are familiar with guns, and we'll fight with you, and do so under your direction. No one wants this mess cleaned up more than we do."

"I can depend on ten men then, if I need them?"

"Yes, you can."

Bart said, "There are three of us out on the Ruby River who have done some fighting. I also have two new men, but I don't know if they'll fight or not."

George sat looking into space. "Then, that makes about fifteen. Well, that's a start. All right, gentlemen, if there is nothing else, I will spend my time right now getting acquainted with the countryside. Bart has offered to take me around today. Who do I report to?"

Everyone pointed to Jim Gray, who said, "I guess it's me. We don't have a formal council, but just a bunch of us who got together because we needed to get something done. You can come to me, and I'll inform the rest. If you need anything, come over and see me and I'll see that you get it. Do you know of anything you need right off?"

"I need a pistol, a rifle and a shotgun. Some of Bart's Indian friends relieved me of mine on the way up. Later, I'll need things like handcuffs, leg irons, paper and pencil, and so on."

Porter Slocum said, "I own the hardware store just down the street. Come in this evening, and I'll have 'em ready for you. Everything but the handcuffs and leg irons. I'll have to order them from somewhere."

The meeting over, Bart led the way to the livery. Once in the saddle, he said, "I think we'll start up at your house and the jail."

They rode on up to the jail, stopped in front, and ground-reined their horses. The jail was a single-story building with stone walls and a shake roof. Bart opened the door and they entered. It opened into a room that he thought must be the office. There was nothing in the room; a door was in the back wall on the left side. Bart went over and looked in. It was a similar-size room with one window at the back. He came back out and saw a hallway on the right side of the front room. It led to a couple of cells with iron bars stretching from floor to ceiling.

Just then, Buster came through the front door. "Well, this is it. How does it look to you?"

He and Bart stood watching while George went through the building. When he came back to the front room, he looked at Buster. "Looks good and solid to me. You've done a good job."

"Thanks. I wanted you to know that the bars are set in solid rock, and they go into heavy timbers on the roof. I don't think anyone will get out."

"Good. It looks solid enough."

After George had satisfied himself with the jail, he and Bart visited the house, and George liked that, as well. It was a small sawed-board cottage. It had a wide, covered porch across the front, with two shuttered windows. Inside, there was a living room, small kitchen, and two small bedrooms.

They got back on their horses and Bart pointed across the street. "That's the court house. The judge comes around every couple of months, and holds court. Down here to the right is Alder Gulch. It was just upstream a short way that they discovered the first gold deposit. Since then, they've torn up the creek bed and surrounding land for several miles." He grinned. "After they get through mining the creek and it clears up, you'll be able to just walk down the hill and throw your line in."

Next, they rode down the hill to Main Street, turned left, and followed the street down the steep hill, Bart pointing out the various stores and buildings as they rode.

When they got to the bottom of the hill and the road leveled out again, George stopped and looked back to where they had just been. "They really hung that town on a hillside, didn't they? Why didn't they just build down here on the flat?"

"I think it's because they first discovered gold in the creek up there and built their first building near the diggings, and it just grew down from there."

Bart put his horse into a lope and they rode on down the valley. Bart kept pointing out diggings where the miners were working their placers in the creek.

Finally, they came to a junction in the road. A few small buildings and one larger one were on the left side. "This is the Alder post office. All that land to the left is our Ruby River Ranch, and that river over there is the Ruby River. That's the fishing hole I promised you. Our headquarters is on the bench the other side of the river."

Bart then reined his horse on down the road. After a couple of miles, they passed through a collection of small buildings. Three saloons, a store, and a collection of small single-story houses stood on the right side of the road. Bart waved his hand in that direction. "This is Nevada City. I don't know much about it, but usually there are some of the more undesirable types hanging around here. I haven't had much to do with anyone here."

He put his horse back into a lope and they went on down the road. A short time later, he stopped on the road and pointed to a large two-story building surrounded by a number of smaller shacks. "This is Robber's Roost. There's a bunch of outlaws here, different ones at different times, but they haven't bothered any of the locals. They seem content to mind their own business and leave others alone. In fact, they even helped us get rid of our last sheriff, and we sell beef to them from the ranch. All of the land you see between here and the river is part of our ranch. In fact, we go on down the river a couple more miles."

"You've given me plenty to chew on for a couple of days. Let me digest that for a while and look around some on my own. Maybe we can get together in a couple days and go over some things."

"Sounds good. I'll ride back with you to the Alder store."

When they reached the store, Bart pulled up. "This is where I get off. Our road takes off right here. Come over any time you feel like it, and the fish in the river are waiting for you. My men and I are available any time you need some help."

"Thanks, I'll give you a holler when I do. Thanks for the tour. I'll see you in a couple of days." He waved, and rode on down the road toward town. Bart finally was able to head for home.

CHAPTER ELEVEN

The sun's rays bounced off the river in a shimmer of light. George Menton, you let that young man talk you into something you swore you'd never do again. He had a very persuasive way about him. Now, it looks like you have bit off a real chunk. It looks like the whole countryside is filled with outlaws of some kind, and you are only one man. Maybe there are ten to a dozen men that would be willing to help you, but none of them are fighting men - mostly storekeepers, and such.

George pulled up his horse and sat watching the young rancher until he had crossed the bridge, then reined his horse on toward town.

As the road began the climb up the hill at the edge of town, two hard-looking characters came down the hill toward him. George moved the reins to his left hand and kept his right hand resting lightly on his thigh, near the pistol and ready to draw if he needed to.

The two glared at him as they passed, and George looked back, staring them down. They averted their eyes, and rode on. George sighed; so it begins! He rode on up to the livery and put away his horse.

Buster Kilgore was in the jail, working yet, when George walked in. "Hello, Sheriff. Man, it is good to say that! I'm just finishing up. The iron is all in place. Mr. Gray brought a desk and a couple of chairs in today. I think you're about in business. All you need now is some prisoners."

George grinned, "I don't think that will be a problem, from all I can see."

"The keys to the cells and to the office are in one of the desk drawers. If you find any problems with the building, give me or Ike a holler. We'll take care of it. See you later."

Buster left, and George sat down at his desk. Now where to start?

Jim gray came in from the back of his store as George entered. "Hello, Sheriff Menton. Are you getting acquainted?"

"I've looked over the country. Thank you for the furniture at the office. Now, I guess I need to know how I feed the inmates when I have some, and I'm going to need one deputy to start with, so that we can have one man watching the jail all the time."

"I'll try to find someone for you and have him up to the jail in the next day or two. I've arranged with Susan over at the café to provide food for the prisoners. She will just bill the town for it. When we find someone to be your deputy, we'll pay his salary. Forty a month should get you a good man."

"Thanks. I've got to say, you all have been a lot more cooperative than any town I've worked for before. I appreciate that."

"We've probably got a worse problem than any of them have had. We'll do what we can to help you."

George took a walk down one side of Main Street, and came back the other. There were four saloons, a bank, two cafes, an opera house, a haberdashery, a hardware store, two grocery/general stores, a saddle shop, boot shop, and in between, about every type of business you could think of designed to take the miners' money as fast as they made it lining both sides of the main street.

Ike's lumber yard was at the bottom of the hill on a side street, and the livery, sheriff's office and jail, the courthouse, and the sheriff's house were on a side street up the hill from Main. The balance of the town was filled with houses, all the way from wood walls with a tent roof to fairly fancy homes, lining the side streets which angled away from Main. All of it was on a steep hillside that sloped away to the north, where Ike's lumberyard was located, and to the south up the hill and over into Alder Creek, where the mines were. He would get his exercise walking this town.

He decided he would make his first round before he turned in. Let the fun begin. He began his rounds on the west edge of town and started along the south side of the road. "Bills Beer Barrel" was the first saloon he came to. It was filled to capacity. George walked in and headed for the bar. The bartender came over to where he was standing. "What'll it be, Mister?"

"Looks like you have a good crowd. What time do you close?"

"When I run out o' customers."

"What's your name?"

"Bill Borgan."

"Are you the owner, Bill?"

"Yes. Mister, you ask a lot of questions. Do you want something to drink, or just a bunch of answers?"

"Bill, I'm the new sheriff, George Menton. Your new closing time is one A.M. It will start tomorrow night."

"That's a laugh. How do you think you're gonna make that stick? We ran the last sheriff out of town on a rail."

"I don't care much for that kind of transportation. One A.M. tomorrow night." He turned and left the building.

George walked on up the hill past the saddle shop and the opera house. Toward the top of the hill, he came to the "Red Garter" saloon. He went in. This was a higher-class establishment. It had roulette wheels, poker tables with padded covers, a piano, and a long bar covered with silver dollars. A large mirror was in back of the bar, with rows of liquor beneath the mirror.

There were ladies of the evening scattered around the tables, mixing with the customers. George went up to the bar and the bartender came over. "Drink, Mister?"

"Are you the owner?"

"No. Sophie Singleton owns the place."

"Would you tell her I would like to see her for a few minutes?"

"One minute." The bartender poured a couple of drinks, and then left the room. Soon, he returned with a very attractive middle-age woman, with dark black hair, and a slim, willowy body. She walked over to where George was standing at the bar. "I'm Sophie, what can I do for you?"

"Sophie, my name is George Menton. I'm the new sheriff. In order to try to get a handle on things around town, we are declaring a curfew at one A.M., starting tomorrow night."

"That applies to all the bars?"

"Yes, and any other businesses."

"Good. You have my support. The town really needs to be cleaned up. We'll close."

"Thanks, Sophie. I appreciate that."

He walked up to the top of the hill, and then back down the other side of the street. He stopped in to the "Brown Palace" and the "Golden Goose" as he went. Both of them had about the same reaction as did Bill's Beer Barrel. Well, now the fat was in the fire. He went back to the hotel and gratefully got undressed and crawled between the sheets.

George lay there, his hands behind his head, going over the night's activities. George, old boy, you've put the bacon in the skillet now. Here comes Oklahoma City, Dallas, Fort Worth, and the rest, all rolled into a ball. You've made your stand, and now the trick is going to be backing it up. All the sand in the world won't be worth a nickel, if the town isn't in back of you. Can you count on them? He guessed there was only one way to find out—try it.

The streets were empty the next morning as George made his way down to Susan's café. It was empty when he walked in the door. He took a table back against the wall, and Susan came out with a cup of coffee in her hand. She set it down on the table.

"I put three fingers of good stuff in there. Figured you'd need it this morning. What would you like for your last meal?"

George grinned. "Word's out already, eh?"

"You couldn't keep a thing like that quiet for five minutes in this town, let alone overnight. Have you lost your mind completely? This town is so full of toughs they could whip an army, and they all like to drink!"

"Well, they'll just have to do it before one A.M. I'll have some of those flapjacks, two eggs, and some bacon."

"The good man upstairs be with you. Flapjacks comin' up"

The store door was standing open when George entered. Jim Gray was standing staring at a shelf behind the counter. He turned when he heard a noise behind him. "Sheriff Menton. I hear you've been busy. I also hear you've lost your mind. How are you going to carry this off?"

"Jim, I'm not a very formal man. Call me George if you would. I'm goin' to carry it off tonight. They're goin' to test me, and if I am to make it stick, I've got to do it alone. Tomorrow night is going to be the test. Tomorrow, they're going to get organized and will be laying for me tomorrow night. This will be the test for the town.

"It's important to show them that the town is behind me. If we don't do that, we've lost the battle. You indicated there were about fifteen men that I could depend on. Can you have them here and armed, shotguns, if possible, tomorrow night about eleven?"

"You expect a gun battle?"

"No, not if they do what I tell them."

"I hope you're right. I'll get them. We'll be here at the store at eleven. One other thing, Buster Kilgore had a bunch of vigilantes that were largely responsible for removing our crooked sheriff several years ago. Maybe he could be helpful to you, as well."

"Thanks, I'll talk to him."

The clanging iron told George that Buster was in his shop. Buster stopped when George entered. "Hello, Sheriff, you're at it early."

"I was just down talking to Jim Gray. He told me that you headed up some vigilantes. Are you still active?"

"No. I haven't seen most of them since we got rid of the old sheriff."

"I don't usually prefer to have any vigilante groups around. They get out of hand so often, but I might need some of them before this is through. This time though, they would be deputized. Can you get them if the need arises?"

"I don't know. As I said, I haven't seen most of them for a couple of years. Some were cattle men, some townspeople, some miners, but I'll look around. It'll take me a while, though."

"I asked Jim to have the fifteen we discussed at the meeting get together tomorrow night with shotguns. I might need some backing then."

"I'll be there."

"All right, Buster, I'll see you then."

# Chapter Twelve

It took a couple of minutes to realize where he was—on his own cot in the big house. He lay there a couple of minutes just soaking in the feeling of being home, and not having thirty miles to ride today. It was great.

He got dressed and made his way to the cook shack. Al and Carmelita were sitting at the table, drinking a cup of coffee. Al pointed to a chair. "Grab a cup, and join us."

Bart poured himself a cup of coffee. "Man, it's good to be home. I've been in that saddle so long I think I'm grown to it."

Carmelita stood. "I'll start breakfast. The rest of them be here shortly."

Al said, "You got here with the new sheriff, all right?"

"Yep, and he's met the council, the jails finished, and he's ready to go."

"What did you think of him? Is he going to be able to do the job?"

"It's a funny thing. When I met him, I almost turned around and came back. He's quiet, friendly, and easy-going. I thought I had the wrong man, or something, but I did see him in a tight, and he was cool as a cucumber. I don't know if any one man is going to be able to put a damper on this mess around here. I think it will depend on how well he can organize the community to stand behind him."

"I think most of this community will stand waaay behind him!"

"If he can get their confidence, he might be able to pull it off. We'll just have to wait and see. How's everything around here?"

"Brandin's done. Holding pasture's fenced, I got a contract to take fifty head of steers to Butte. We got one-hundred-and-fifty-dollars each for them. Slim and the boys are workin' on the bull pasture fence now."

"Sounds like I need to be gone more often. You get more done when I'm not here."

"Oh, no! I'll run the cattle end of this deal; you take care of the business. I grew fourteen grey hairs for every inch of scalp I have while you were traipsin' off."

"When do we have to have the steers in Butte? We're goin' to be lookin' at snow one of these days."

I was thinkin' of startin' them up there this week."

"How are the two new hands workin' out?"

"They're fine, both hard workers. They've never been on a drive before. That might make it interesting. They do learn pretty fast, though."

Slim, Bear, and Shorty came in from outside. Everyone said their hellos and Carmelita brought the food to the table. When they had finished eating, Bart asked everyone to stay a minute.

"Boys, I brought back the sheriff that the town wanted. I think he's going to be all right, but he's going to need help. I promised him that we would give him any help he needed from us. I can't order you to take up your guns and go after the outlaws, and I'll not think any less of you if you don't want to. I want to know, though, whether you will or not, so I can tell Menton how much help we can give him."

Al said, "You know you have mine."

Slim said, "I ride for the brand."

The other two both indicated a willingness to go along.

"I thought as much, and told Menton I thought we would have this many to help him. Al, did you make any contacts to get cut-meat orders? I'm going to go back to town today. I need to let Menton know we're going to be gone a week, or a little better, driving those steers, and need to get an idea from him when he might be wanting us."

"No, I didn't get any of that done."

"Well, if I get time I'll explore that a little."

"Give Menton a kiss for us if she's home."

"Maybe I'd better take the wagon and get supplies for the drive."

"Why don't we just take some jerky and hardtack in our saddlebags, instead? It's only a two-day drive. It'll go a lot faster if we don't have to fool with the wagon."

Bart looked at the other three. "You game for that?"

They all nodded their heads. He rose to go. "All right, that's what we'll do then. I'll pick up some jerky and hardtack while I'm in there."

Two riders were ahead of him as he started up the hill into Virginia City. Bart urged the horse on a little faster to try to get a better look at them. They rode right on past the stores, the hotel, and the saloons. They were headed right on through the business section of town. What were they up to? It looked like some of the bunch that had been hanging around. Maybe they were leaving the country. That would be a good thing. He reined into the haberdashery and tied the horse to the hitch rack.

Ruby came out to meet him. Bart met her at the top of the steps. He took her in his arms. "The boys said to kiss you for them, but I think I'll do it for me, first." Which he did.

They sat down on the steps to talk. Bart said, "I hate to tell you this, but I've got to take another trip."

"What is it this time? Do you have to find the general of the army, and bring him here?"

"No, Al sold a bunch of steers and we have to deliver them to Butte. We'll be back in about four days, if everything goes all right."

"Oh, all right. I guess I'd better get used to it. I think you have a condition. It's called itchy-foot. It never stays still."

"Well, with enough incentive I just might stay home. Let's go get married right now, and I'll never leave again."

"No, you don't! Ginny and I have been talking. We're going to have church weddings, with all the trimmings."

"That sounds scary."

"When are you leaving?"

"In the morning. That is, unless George needs us. I told him we would help if he did."

"Oh, Bart, when is all this going to end?"

"Not until we get this rough bunch out of the country. They're never going to let it rest. Ruby, I've got to find George, and see how he's doing. He may need our bunch in here, and that means I need to ride back out to the ranch and then back here. I need to go."

"All right, if you have to. Kiss me."

The door to the sheriff's office was open, and Bart walked in. The new sheriff was sitting at the desk, laying out ammunition for the new guns he had on the desk. He looked up as Bart entered.

"Hello, Bart. I'm glad you're here. I need to talk to you."

"Hello, George. What's up?"

"Tonight's the night. I'm going to need some help. I gave the bars a curfew last night; tonight, they're going to test me. I've got to do this one alone. They've got to know that I'm protecting the town. I can bluff them tonight, but tomorrow night they'll be organized and I'll need the town behind me then, and with me. After that, I can handle it with one deputy."

"They're a pretty tough bunch. George, are you sure?"

"Well, you're never sure, but it usually works out that way. If you don't get your bluff in, you've lost the ball game."

"All right. We'll be here tomorrow night. Now I've got to go sell some meat. See you then."

"Thanks, Bart."

Bart spent the rest of the afternoon visiting cafes, bars, and the meat market, setting up a schedule for delivering meat to them, and a price for the product.

When he had finished, he rode down the hill toward the ranch. He saw some miners running a placer hose, and stopped to watch them. The men were stretching their muscles to the limit, holding that stream of water into the bank while they were standing in freezing water. Others were shoveling the mud into the sluice box, trying to find a few flakes of gold at a time, and always hoping that that great big nugget would find its way in there, as well.

And then, what did they do? Many of them just went to the bar and spent it on liquor, or cards, or what have you, and then they went back the next day and did it all over again. You had to wonder what it was all about. He guessed it might not be a lot worse than riding through blizzards, rainstorms, and what have you, to get some dumb cow out of a mud pond, or get her up when she lay down with her back downhill and couldn't get up again. He rode on down the hill and across the river to the ranch.

That evening, he asked everyone to stay after supper. "I talked to our new sheriff today. He put a one A.M curfew on the bars last night, and tonight he's going around to them and trying to make it stick. He said he could do it alone tonight, but wanted us to be there tomorrow night. We'll have to wait until day after tomorrow to leave with the steers."

Slim laughed. "How big is thet there sheriff? He must be taller'n a tree, and bigger'n a hill! Thet's one tough bunch thet hangs around there."

"You wouldn't know it to look at him, but he is one tough hombre, too. If there's anyone who can pull it off, it'll be Menton."

It was pitch dark, and the light was shining through the door onto the boardwalk, as George walked into Bill's Beer Barrel saloon. It looked as if there were about ten men standing at the bar. Most of the tables were full of card players. The bartender was at one of the tables bringing bottles of beer to the players. He saw George, and froze.

Suddenly, the room became deadly quiet. George walked over and leaned against the bar, his pistol side away from the wood.

He stood staring at the crowd, and waited until the bartender returned to the bar.

George said, "It's time to announce that this is the last round of drinks."

'You can't make that stick. They won't stand for it!"

"Your job is to tell them. I'll worry about them standing for it. Now, do it!"

The bartender made the announcement, and there was a general growling among the customers. The toughs at the bar moved away enough to confront George. The leader made a step toward George.

"There ain't a man in the world could make us quit drinkin' 'til we get ready, and you sure couldn't."

"The lights are goin' out in here in five minutes, and you are all going out the door. Now, I can't kill all of you, but you will be the first one, the next four will be those right beside you, and the sixth one will get it right between the eyes. Now drink up, and start moving."

George stood there staring the leader in the eyes, his hand on the handle of his gun.

The leader stared back at George, until finally he had to look away. He looked at the others. "Aw, come on. I've had all the beer I could drink anyway." He turned and left through the door, and the others followed after him. Then the tables emptied, and the bartender looked at George. "I'll be damned; I never would have believed it!"

George turned to follow the others out. "Go ahead and close up. Do the same thing tomorrow night."

Sophie had the Red Garter closed by the time he walked by, so he crossed the street to the Brown Palace. Sam Cody had already told everyone that it was closing time, and some of them had started to leave. George went in and stood by the bar, and the patrons began getting up and leaving, amid grumbling and dark glances. Before long, the place was empty.

Sam came over to where George was standing. "I didn't think they would go, but once you came in, I guess they decided that it was the best thing to do. I think I can make it stand, now."

"Good, glad we didn't have any trouble. They may try a little harder tomorrow night, but we have to make it stand right from the start. See you tomorrow night."

That left one. The Golden Goose was the last one on that side of the street. George made his way there. It was still going full steam. Some of the bunch from the first saloon were in there now and talking to a group standing at the bar. This was going to be tougher.

George walked up and stood by the bar. The same man that had led the bunch at the other bar came a few steps toward George. "You chased us out of the other bar, but we still have some drinkin' to do. We're not leavin' this time."

Several of the others moved up beside the leader, hands hovering over their guns. One of them spoke up. "We're all stayin', lawman. We're not goin' to be pushed around. You can just pack up and leave."

"My first bullet has a place in the middle of your forehead, the next one in his." George pointed to the leader, and as he brought his arm back from pointing, he swiftly dropped it to his pistol and brought it up, training it on the second man. It caught them by surprise, and they stood staring at the muzzle of the gun. They remained looking at the gun while George continued to look into the eyes of the second man.

The leader made a grab for his gun and George planted a bullet between the man's feet. The man jumped back, leaving his gun in his holster. The man told his companions, "Let's rush him, he can't shoot us all."

George quickly put a bullet into the large light above their heads, and glass showered down on them. They all ducked, and tried to get out from under the falling glass. George shot into the floor at their feet twice more.

"The next bullets aren't goin' to go into the floor. You'd better leave while you still can!"

Amid much grousing, the men filed out of the building. As he went through the door, the leader shouted, "This ain't over, lawman. You'll get yours."

George waited until the bartender had closed the doors and turned out the lights. George reached back to his gunbelt and replaced the spent bullets in his gun. Then, he slipped out the back door, in case there was a welcoming committee waiting outside in the street. Then he went down side streets to his office, and lay down on his cot in the back room.

When the last man had entered the room, Jim Gray opened the meeting. "Gents, you all know why we're here. I'm going to give you one last chance to bow out. We know it's going to be dangerous, and a good chance some of us might not come back, but if you're goin' to back out, now is the time to do it. We don't want Sheriff Menton to go in there depending on backup, and discover he doesn't have any. I'll turn the meeting over to him, now."

Nobody moved and George walked up in front of the men. "The saloons have been shut down at one o'clock as of last night. They left fairly peaceably for the most part, if not also agreeably, but tonight will be different. They have had a long night and all day to think about it, and there will be trouble tonight.

"Here's the way I want to do it. I want one man to come into the saloon with me. Bart Madison. I know he can handle a gun, if it becomes necessary. Next, I want ten of you to stand outside the door, half on one side, the other half on the opposite side. When they come out, have your guns at the ready, and if they throw their guns on you, shoot. Be sure they are intending to fight you, though.

"The other five men, I want to do the same thing on the back door. If shooting erupts inside, besides a few warning shots by me, come in ready to fight. We'll start at the Beer Barrel. Sophie will have The Red Garter closed. I think the Brown Palace will be closed, and then we'll wind up at the Golden Goose, and we may have trouble there. They're the ones that gave me the most trouble last night. Are there any questions?"

Henry Ferguson asked, "Are we gonna shoot to kill?"

"Yes. Any lawman will tell you: don't shoot until you have to, and if you have to, shoot to kill. It could mean your life. All right, let's get to it."

The group discussed the situation until time to leave. They then walked down to the Beer Barrel saloon. The men split up, lining up at each side of the doorways, and George and Bart went in. George walked to the bar. Bart followed closely, stepping to the side of the doorway, with his back to the wall where he could watch every part of the room while George talked. "All right, bartender, it's time for last drinks."

The bartender called out, "Last drinks. Drink up. Closing time!"

There was some call for drinks, but the usual small group stood in a circle talking to each other. George stood ready, watching them.

Finally, the same spokesman from the previous night stepped out in front of the others. "Sheriff, you called the shots last night, but tonight it'll be different. We ain't goin' nowhere. We're stayin' here 'til we decide when we want to quit drinkin', and there's nothin' you can do about it."

"Oh, there's plenty I can do about it. The only question is: how far do you want me to go before you leave."

They all drew their pistols and the leader said, "Yuh see, lawman, yuh now have ten pistols in your face. They're already drawn, and you don't have a chance of beatin' us."

The leader started to raise his pistol, and Bart shot it out of his hands. The man cursed loudly.

George said, "Now, the rest of you put those things away and go home. We don't want any further trouble. If you folks can't drink all you need to by one in the morning, take a big drink of water before you come."

A man near the back of the group started to raise his pistol, but before he could get his gun all the way up, George had drawn his gun and shot the man in the shoulder. The man's gun went flying across the floor.

George said, "All right, now start moving toward the door. Quitting time is one in the morning. That's not a problem for anyone, and things will be a lot easier if you just decide that is the way things are. No one has been killed, and there is no need for that to happen. Now, move!"

The men stood staring at George, and then, looking at Bart, standing by the door, began to move slowly in that direction, with many dire threats coming from the group.

As they went through the door, they had to walk between the armed townspeople, and they started moving even faster. They soon dispersed, and went on their way.

The Red Garter was closed, as was the Brown Palace. The Golden Goose was still going, but quickly cleared out and closed when George and Bart came in.

George told the townspeople, "I want to thank you men. I couldn't have done it without you. I think I can handle it now for the time being. They know you mean business. There will be instances in the future where one or two of them will want to make a stand, but I think I can handle that. If it gets serious again, I may have to call on you once more."

Slim walked up and shook George's hand. "Sheriff, you've got more guts than a lion with a chunk of meat in his mouth! I wanta shake yer hand."

Jim looked over the bunch. "I think that goes for all of us. You have our thanks. If you need us again, we'll be ready."

It was near noon the next morning when George made his way to Susan's Cafe. He took a seat at the back of the room. Susan, herself, came out of the kitchen when she saw him come in.

"Good morning, Sheriff. I heard you had quite a ruckus last night."

"It was a start."

"What'll it be this morning?"

"Pancakes, eggs, and ham, if you have it."

"For you, anything under the sun." She went back into the kitchen, and came back with a cup of coffee. "Thought you might need this to wash it down."

George watched her as she left the room. Susan was a flaxen-haired woman, slim and pretty, with a killer smile, and always cheerful. He just might have to eat here more often.

He sat thinking about last night's work, and where he had to go from here. He'd start his rounds today, getting people used to seeing him around town, and then continue with the bars tonight. He felt pretty good about his progress - things were going pretty much as they should.

Flora, one of the waitresses, brought George's meal, which he finished with relish, and when he walked up to the counter to pay, Susan stuck her head out of the kitchen door. "The meal's on the house. You're the best news we've had in a long time."

George grinned. "Thanks very much. It was really good." He was still grinning as he walked out the door. Not only was she pretty, she was one heck of a good cook.

CHAPTER THIRTEEN

The steers were all gathered in the holding pasture. Bart, Al, Slim, Bear, and Shorty had packed their saddlebags with jerky, hardtack, and whatever other foodstuffs they could cram in that would survive a ride.

Bart tied his lasso to his saddle horn and turned to the rest. "These steers are gonna be harder to drive than the herd we brought up from Texas. They're young and frisky and won't hold together like an older bunch of cattle." He grinned. "I think what we'll do is have Slim lead that old roan bull again, and the others will follow him."

Slim bellowed out, "No! No, yuh don't! I'm not goin' to be on the other end of a rope with that moss-backed, wrinkle-horned ladino. I'll shoot him first, and then shoot muhself!"

Al laughed. "Shucks, Slim. That old bull loves you so much you could just walk on down the road in front and he'd just walk right behind you. Why I remember down in the holding pas—"

"No, yuh don't," Slim exploded. "Yuh don't talk about thet!"

Bear asked, "What happened in the holdin' pasture?"

Slim blew out a great breath. "Some folks're jest workin' their jaws, and some folks are goin' to get a busted jaw if they keep it up!"

Al tried to suppress a snicker. "Aw, Slim, I just thought they might enjoy a good 'belly' laugh."

A great groan came out of Slim's throat, and he stamped his foot on the ground in frustration.

Bart said, "Enough. Let's get on with it. I want Al and Bear to ride forward, Slim leading out front, and Shorty and I'll ride drag and keep 'em movin'. We'll drive 'em down the road, and try to get across the Jefferson today. Then we should be able to make Butte early tomorrow. Probably, our toughest job will be getting them across the bridges. Let's go."

The bridge across the Ruby was their first challenge. They got them turned down the road after getting out of the holding pasture, but when they got to the bridge, the steers didn't want to get on it. The holding pasture fence kept them on the road on that side, but many of them sprinted away on the other side and had to be turned and brought back to the herd.

By slowly keeping the pressure on them, a few steers finally braved getting on the bridge, and after a few tentative steps, started on across. Then the rest followed and they were soon across the river.

They next had to turn them onto the main road and, after several skirmishes, they were once more heading in the desired direction. Things went fairly smoothly then for a while. There was only an occasional sprint after a lone steer that wanted to get away.

As they came into the town of Nevada City, the steers became more nervous. It was harder to hold them in a tight bunch. One made a dash to the right, and Bart put his horse after it. The animal ran past a house and turned behind it, Bart after it at a full gallop. Just before he reached the house, he heard a gunshot. As he rounded the back corner of the house, he saw two men standing there, one with a smoking pistol in his hand.

Bart drew his pistol and had it pointed at the two men as he brought his horse to a sliding stop. The steer was lying on the ground, obviously dead. Bart kept his gun trained on the two men. "Looks like you just bought yourself a steer."

The man with the gun started to turn it toward Bart. Bart moved his gun to dead-center on the man. "Don't try it."

The man lowered his gun. "Who are you, and what are you doin' here?"

"I'm the guy that used to own that steer; now it's yours. And I'm looking for pay for it."

"You're outta your head. We're not payin' for anything."

"You are. And now." Bart knew he couldn't delay, he had to get back to the herd. He took off his hat, still holding the gun on the two. "Put away that gun first, unbuckle your belts and drop 'em. Then put everything in your pockets in this hat. I want those pockets inside out when you're through."

Grudgingly, the men complied. First one and then the other put the contents of their pockets in Bart's hat. Bart laid it on his lap. "Now, pick up those gunbelts and bring 'em here, slow-like."

When this was done, Bart said, "Now sit down and take off your boots and throw 'em over that bush there." Again, the two were slow to comply and their looks threw daggers Bart's way, but in the end, they did as they were told.

Bart whirled his horse and galloped to join the herd. At least, it would take them a little time to reach another gun of some kind.

Dust boiled up from the animal's hooves, covering Shorty and Bart with a fine layer of whitish dust. It got in their mouths, their eyes and nose, until it almost gagged them. Bart rode out to the side of the road as much as he could to get out of the thickest cloud, and when he could get a look at Shorty, he was doing the same.

They passed Robber's Roost, and there was no activity to be seen from the two-story house nestled just below the roadway. Bart couldn't help thinking what an irony it was. The place always looked so peaceful, and yet it housed some of the most notorious outlaws in the west. As Sundance had told him, they liked to keep it that way and not attract a lot of lawmen down their way.

As they progressed down the road, the steers became more and more used to traveling together and there were fewer instances when one of them made a dash for the brush to the side of the road.

They didn't stop for lunch, but kept the steers moving and each rider reached back into his saddlebags for some jerky and hardtack, followed by more swigs from their canteens. That evening, as the sun's rays were casting their longest shadows, they came to the twin bridges over the Jefferson. As before, the steers were reluctant to get on the bridge, but after the first one made a bold attempt, the rest followed without incident.

They found a grassy meadow beside the river, where they called a halt. Bart set up a night-herd schedule, and those not on the first shift ate their meal of hardtack and jerky, and soon were in their soogans to try to get some sleep before it was their turn to ride around the herd.

As daylight crept down onto the distant hills to the west, the crew climbed out of their soogans, grabbed another cold meal, and started the steers on north.

As the day progressed, the terrain became steeper, sagebrush gave way to juniper, and the ground became rocky. They had to stop every so often to give their horses a chance to catch their breath, and the steers showed no desire to run off while they waited. Many of them lay down in the road while they were stopped.

The sun was reaching its zenith when they topped a tall ridge. The ground was almost entirely rock, and juniper trees were bravely trying to find a place to put their roots in the cracks in the rock. Bart looked ahead and could see the City of Butte perched at the top of a mountain ahead of them. A mountain valley dropped off from the city to a more level area further down the mountainside.

Al rode back to where Bart was sitting his horse. "That valley down there is where I understood they wanted the cattle. I can see a corral down there. We should head for that."

"You've got the lead. Let's do it."

When they got the steers to a point right above the corrals, Al signaled to Bart he was going down the hill. Slim reined his horse to the center of the road and turned the steers down the hill. Al plunged down the steep hillside and had enough time to open one of the corral gates before the cattle got there.

It was only a short time until all of them were in the corral, and the riders were standing by their horses, feeling good about getting the job done. The corral owner came out to meet them. Al stepped forward to speak to him. "Mr. Cranston?"

"Yes, are you Al Allen?"

"Yes. Here are your steers. We lost one on the way."

"They look to be in good shape. Where are you staying tonight?"

"We'll find a hotel uptown."

"I'd recommend the Nugget Hotel. The beds are mostly clean, and they have a dining room in the building. They're as reasonable as any of 'em."

"Thanks. This is my partner, Bart Madison. This is Slim Carson, Bear Grant, and Shorty Jackson."

"Glad to meet you fellows. You must be tired. I'll get together with you in the morning at the hotel, and get you paid then. You made better time than we thought, your stock is in good condition, and we hope to do business with you again. Tonight's lodging and meal is on the Butte Land and Livestock Company. I'll see you tomorrow." The man turned back into the office building beside the corrals.

They found a road winding up the steep hillside to the town. The livery was on the east side of town, and they made arrangements for the care of their horses, then, looked for the hotel.

The town was located at the summit of a steep hill. Mining shafts were interspersed with the buildings all over town, streets ran in every direction, and small, tall, narrow, and wide buildings were side by side throughout the town. Some buildings had wooden sidewalks in front of them, the next one would not. Some had porches across the front, some had wood siding, some brick, some were tents, and all were busy, with people going in and out, going about their business. It was not like a town any of them had ever seen before.

A two-story wooden building was down the street ahead of them, and when they were close enough to read the sign it said, 'THE NUGGET'. They went in and arranged for their rooms, and by the time they had washed up, the dining room was open.

They entered the room and found chairs that had been placed beside four long tables. The cook's helpers were soon coming in with platters of beef, potatoes, ham, vegetables, and bread, and large pots of coffee.

They fell to with gusto. When the platters were emptied, they were quickly refilled. Before the Ruby River crew had hardly started to eat, the dining room was filled with miners, and the talk was mostly about ore quality, length of mining shafts, and other bits of mining information.

When they had finished their meal, the cook's helpers topped it all off with apple pie.

Slim sat back, and rubbed his stomach. "Thet was th' best throat-tickling chuck I've had in a month o' Sundays. I might jest set here'n grow old."

There was agreement from the entire group. Bart stood. "All of you come on up to my room. I want to talk to you."

When they had assembled in the room, he said, "I didn't want to talk about money down there in the crowd. I know some of you might want to see some of the night life here in town. I can't give you much until we get paid tomorrow, but here's an advance of twenty dollars each toward your pay. Maybe that'll buy you a few drinks, anyhow."

He handed out the money, and all but Al trooped off to see the sights.

Bart put the remainder of the money in his money belt. "Are you wanting to lay over for a day, or would you rather head back tomorrow?"

"Why don't we lay over a day? The boys have been pretty much having their noses to the grindstone for a long time. It might do them good to blow off a little steam."

"All right. I'll go down and pay for an extra day for the rooms. Then, why don't we go down and join 'em for a drink, or two, before hittin' the hay?"

The first saloon they found after leaving the hotel was 'The Miners' Oasis'. Bart turned in at the swinging doors. "This is probably where they stopped. It's the first one down the street."

The room was jumping. A long bar extended the length of the room in front of them. Miners and others stood elbow to elbow down its entire length. A piano was going full blast against the wall to their right. The rest of the room was filled with tables placed so close together that there was barely room to walk between the people seated at them. Nearly every table was filled with customers, and dancehall girls were hanging over many shoulders.

They did spot an empty table by the near wall to their right. They wound their way to it, and took a seat.

Before long, a barmaid in a skimpy skirt came to their table. "What'll you have, boys?"

"Beer."

"Same."

She left, and Bart stood to survey the room to see if he could see the Ruby River hands. Finally, he saw Slim sitting at a table talking to some miners. He couldn't tell if the others were with him, or not. He sat back down.

"Slim, at least, is over there at a table. I couldn't tell if the others are with him, or not. Let's have our beer and then go see 'em."

"Slim never met anyone who wasn't a friend. He'd make friends with a grizzly if the bear would stay still long enough."

The barmaid brought their beer and Bart paid her. Then they sat watching the crowd and enjoying the cool liquid. When they had finished, they got up and walked over to the table where Slim and the others were sitting.

Slim got up and found a couple of chairs for them and brought them to the table. "Sit down, fellers. Yuh need to talk to this man. His name's Jake Hardin. Jake, these are my bosses, Bart Madison and Al Allan. They own the Ruby River Ranch. Jake, here's, a miner. He works in that big'n we saw at the top of the hill."

Bart held out his hand. "Glad to know you, Jake."

Slim said, "Jake, tell 'em what yuh was tellin' us."

Jake looked around before talking. "I was just tellin' Slim that there was a rough bunch that had been raisin' hell with the businesses here in Butte for the last year, and now have mostly moved out. I was told that they had plans to move into your area. There's a town called Nevada or Colorado, or somethin' like that, where a bunch of outlaws have moved into. From what I was told, they intend to take over that mining town near there, run out the storekeepers, and hold the miners hostage for their supplies, tools and what have you, for whatever price they wanta ask.

"They did that in some mining town in California, and finally ran the miners out, because they couldn't afford their prices. They're a tough bunch, and pretty well organized. They've been leavin' Butte in small bunches over the last year, or so. I wondered if you had been having trouble with 'em."

"We've had quite a few tough-looking characters come through town, and have had some trouble with them. How many would you say have moved over there?"

"Well, I don't have any way o' knowin' that, but I'd guess there's somewhere between thirty and fifty of 'em. I heard one of 'em say there was no law down there, now, and it'd be easy pickin's."

Bart started to tell him that they might be surprised about the law, but then decided to keep his own counsel. Surprise might be their best defense.

After some more talk about the benefits of placer and hard-rock mining, Bart took his leave of the group. Al and the others decided to do the town before turning in. On the way back to the hotel, Bart wondered how many of them he'd have to bail out of jail in the morning. Maybe their twenty-dollar limit would keep some of them sober. He left a seven o'clock call at the desk, and went to bed.

The next morning after he had eaten, he came down to the lobby to wait for John Cranston. They hadn't set a time, but he guessed Cranston had to wait for the bank to open to get their money. He was just anxious to get it over with.

It was nearly ten-thirty when Cranston finally arrived. He shook Bart's hand. "Sorry this is so late, but the bank doesn't open until ten. Is there somewhere we can do this that's not so public?"

"Let's go up to my room. We should be all right there."

When they got to the room and were seated, Cranston opened his satchel and pulled out a roll of money. "That was fifty steers at one hundred dollars, right?"

"That's what Al said the arrangement was."

Cranston counted out five thousand dollars. "There you are. Please count it yourself."

Bart took the roll of bills and counted them. "That's not correct. We only delivered forty-nine steers. We lost one on the way."

"That's all right. You delivered them ahead of schedule, and they're in better shape than we expected. They're better quality than we usually get. Keep the extra, and I hope we can do business again."

"You bet. We'll be glad to do this any time."

They shook hands again. Cranston picked up his satchel, and said, "You'll be hearing from us. Good day, Mr. Madison."

Bart closed the door and sat down at the table. He separated enough money from the roll of bills to pay the men their wages for the month, and put the rest in his money belt. As he was getting ready to go down to the dining room, there was a knock on the door. Bart called, "Come in," and Al walked in and sat down.

He looked pretty good, Bart thought, for a night of carousing. "Well, did you do the town last night?"

"No, I sat there for a little bit, had another beer, and came back here. The rest were goin' strong, though, when I left."

"It's amazing how far twenty dollars'll go."

"I think the miners were buying most of the drinks. They were all feeling pretty fine when I left. Bart, what are you going to do today? I think the rest are probably still in bed."

"I thought I'd walk around town a little, and look it over. Why?"

"If I can get some money, I want to get Carmelita a ring. After all the talk about weddings and things, she's wanting one, I know. I thought I'd surprise her and then look up a preacher when we get back."

"I was wondering if you two were ever going to tie the knot. We'll get the other bedroom in the big house ready."

"We're getting the ranch on pretty good footing now, aren't we?"

"Really good, and it will be a lot better, too. I think we'll keep this market going, and we can probably sell this many steers at a time here from now on. Also, I was able to get some pretty good sales for the cut meat in Virginia City. We'll do all right."

"Carmelita and I have been talking, and we would like to build a house of our own—probably across the road from the big house."

"Let's hold out a thousand of this beef money for ranch expenses. That should hold us until the next beef shipment, and we'll be gettin' money from the cut meat to keep operating on. About one hundred fifty for the wages - that should leave thirty five hundred. Take that for the house, and get Ike started on it."

"I can't take all that. Half of that is yours."

"I have a house that was half yours, and I've some saved for the furniture I need, the ranch pays for my food - what else would I need? Here, you take it. I kept out enough so that, with what I had already, I can buy a couple of rings that I need. Let's go see a jeweler."

After a great deal of agony, trying to pick out suitable rings for their soon-to-be spouses, the two made their selections and left the store.

They spent the rest of the day walking the town, looking at some of the mines scattered throughout, and then returned to the hotel in time to eat supper. The rest of the crew soon joined them.

Slim looked the same as ever - jovial, friendly, and ready to roll. Bear and Shorty seemed as if maybe last night's celebration might have been more than they were used to. They seemed a little drug-out, and ready for a night's rest.

Bart paid them the rest of their wages from the money he had received from Cranston. "Here you go, boys. Thought you might want the rest of this month's wages so you could have it while you were here in town."

Slim said, "Whoeee! I'm gonna holler tonight! Whiskey, women, and poker, here I come!"

Bear looked at him, red-eyed. "Not me. I have a date with that bed upstairs."

Shorty nodded agreement.

Bart said, "Do whatever suits you. We leave at sunrise in the morning. Be ready then."

The liveryman was still sleeping in the tack room when the Ruby River gang arrived. He quickly got out of bed and was up with them by the time they were saddled. Bart paid him for taking care of the horses, and they started off down the hill toward home.

They stopped to rest the horses and eat lunch at the Jefferson River bridge. As they sat on the river bank watching the water, Bart asked, "We're makin' good time; do you want to try to make home tonight, or ease up and overnight along the way?"

Al said, "Home." Shorty and Bear said, "Home." Slim said, "I'll be hornswoggled if I stay out here all alone. Hey, did you fellers see that mine up on top? It had a long, high ladder with a wheel on top and a wire rope big enough to strangle a frog. Them crazy galoots ride that thing miles down inta the ground to go ta work! I allus thought that cowpunchers needed half a brain more to be half smart, but them boys got us beat seventeen ways to Sunday!"

Shorty said, "Not only that, they got candles on their hats! They could singe their whiskers, if a good wind came along."

Bear chimed in. "The noise'd get me. I'll sit and listen to a cow bawlin' any day."

Bart swallowed that last bit of hardtack he'd taken out of his saddlebags, and stood. "If you all are through tellin' how tough the miners have it, why don't we climb on the hurricane deck and head for home."

The sun was low in the west when they passed by Robber's Roost. It was quiet, as usual, with only a horse tied to the hitch rack for visible life around the place. Bart had to wonder if the influx of toughs from Butte had any connection with the outlaws down there. There sure wasn't any sign of it. That miner did say they were headed for Nevada City, however.

Darkness lowered to the ground as they were coming into the outskirts of Nevada City. Lights were starting to come on in many of the buildings. He couldn't see any signs of large gatherings of people. He had ridden through many small towns in his life, but this one always gave him a crawly feeling, almost as if it was just sitting waiting for some disaster.

Just as they were leaving town, two men walked toward them from the house where the steer had been shot. They stood in the road as the group approached. In the dark, Bart couldn't tell if they were the ones who had shot the steer, or not.

Bart moved over and put his horse to a trot to get between the men and his crew, just in case. One of the men in the road held up a hand, "Stop, I need to talk to yuh."

The crew brought their horses to a stop, then the man said, "Have any of you got some makin's? We've plumb run out."

Slim reached in his pocket and pulled out his Bull Durham. He threw the bag to the man.

Suddenly, both men on the ground had their guns pointed at Bart and the rest. "All right, hand over all the cash you have. We know you sold a bunch o' cattle so you have to have a potful. The first one who makes a move for his gun will be the first one dead!"

Bart said, "These boys don't have any money. I've got it right here. Just don't shoot."

The man looked up. "Charley, look who we have here. This is the tough guy that took our guns. I wonder what we should do about that."

"I think maybe we should do the same to him, take his boots, and then see if we could have a little fun."

Bart said, "You don't have any quarrel with the others, let them go. We'll talk about the rest when they're gone. I've got the money right here in my saddle bag."

He reached into the saddle bag and brought out a small sack he had in there, then leaned down with his left hand and handed it down toward the nearest outlaw. The man reached out to take the bag. Just as it was touching the man's hand, Bart dropped it, and it fell to the ground. The man automatically looked down to where it fell. Bart pulled his gun and held it in front of the man's face. "Now, it's time for you to give me that gun."

The other outlaw brought his gun up to aim at Bart, when there was a shot and the man's gun flew to the ground.

Smoke rose from Slim's gun, and he kept it trained on the outlaw's face. "Mister, thet ain't a healthy thing t' do. I usually try to get at least one skunk every day, and I ain't had the chance yet today."

Bart looked down at the first man. "Hand me your gun, then step back a pace."

When he had the gun, he waved it at the other outlaw. "Now, the both of you walk back over to that house. If you stop, I don't think I can keep Slim from getting his skunk quota. Now, move!"

When the men reached the house, Bart put the spurs to his horse, and the group rode on down the road toward home.

CHAPTER FOURTEEN

George Menton sat down at his desk, heavily. He was bone-tired. Before breakfast this morning, there had been a squabble out in the street between a couple of miners. It had taken him longer than it should have to break it up. Then he had gone into Susan's for breakfast. The place had been packed, and he had had to share a table with a couple of miners. Susan had been so busy in the kitchen that she never came out. George felt a real sense of disappointment.

Two saloon fights had made the morning rounds go faster, and then there had been the stand-off with a couple of toughs in the afternoon. He had had to throw both of them in jail before it was through. His jail was about full! They were packed like apples in a tub in there, and the need for more room wasn't letting up. He'd better talk to Jim Gray. Something had to happen. The prisoners were so crowded that they were sitting on the floor, or standing.

Throughout the day as he had made his rounds, George could spot strangers making their way through town, some standing on corners, seemingly watching a store front, or loitering in front of a store window. He wasn't sure how he knew they were strangers, but there was something about them that tickled George's sheriff sense.

Jim looked up as George entered the store.

"Evening, George, how's it going?"

"Hello, Jim. Everything's under control, but we're out of room at the jail. I've got to turn some loose, or get more room. We've got outlaws, fist fighters, gunslingers, drunks, and everything else all shoved together in the two cells. There isn't anything but standing room in there. I'm going to turn some of the ones with lesser crimes loose, but that's just a short- term solution."

"Well, let me know. I'll get the council together, if we need to do something else."

"Jim, there's another matter. We've had a series of robberies. Somehow, the robber or robbers seem to know where I am, and when there's no one watching the stores. These outlaws seem to be coming from somewhere away from town. I don't see how they could know unless there was someone here tipping them off. I've tried to change my times when I make the rounds, tried taking a different route and everything I can think of, and they still seem to know where I am, and when."

"What can we do? Do you need more help from us, and do we need to add on to the jail? By the way, I have found a Deputy for you and he'll be to work in the morning. He's an out of work ranch hand and says he can handle a gun. His name is Jack Billings."

"That's great! He can watch the jail. Let's hold off a little while on the other help. For a town this size, the jail should be plenty big. We've got something going on here that's unusual. There're more thugs around than should be, and they seem to be waiting for someone, or something. I've noticed almost every day that there are a couple of them that go into that apothecary up there at the end of the street. I suppose they could be getting medicine for someone, but it sure seems to be a regular thing. I'll keep my eye on them."

"I wouldn't think that the owner would have anything to do with an outlaw bunch. He's showed himself to be a withering coward."

"Well, I'll watch for a while, anyhow. See you later."

Just then, Ruby came into the room. "Wasn't that Sheriff Menton, Dad? Is something wrong?"

"No, he was just discussing the overcrowding at the jail."

"I'm going over to Ginny's for a while. I won't be long."

"I wish you wouldn't go out this late. You know there are ruffians out there all the time anymore. Wait 'til I close up, and I'll walk you over."

"Oh, it's just a little ways over there. I'll only be out there a minute. I'll be all right." She kissed him on the cheek and went out the door.

She hurried eagerly down the walk. It was such fun sitting with Ginny and talking over wedding plans, future plans, and in general, just being together. Ginny was such a good friend. She was going to miss being able to pop out the front door and, in just a minute, be with Ginny, after she moved to the ranch.

Suddenly, she was grabbed from behind, and someone was dragging her into a space between a couple of buildings. She screamed, and tried to fight him back.

The man pushed her down onto the ground, and she could feel the sharp rocks poking into her back. She screamed again, and he hit her in the face.

"Do that again, and I'll knock you out. Now lay still."

He held her down, straddling her, and ran a hand down along her face. It felt horrible, and she shuddered.

"What are you doing to me? Let me go!"

"Oh, I'll let you go, but not just yet." He put his hands around her neck and then brought them forward. "I haven't been with a girl like you for a long time. You are prettier than a peach."

He bent over, trying to kiss her. She turned her head and screamed again. He hit her with his fist. "I told you not to do that!"

Her jaw felt like it was broken. It hurt something awful. She clenched her fists and started pounding him in the face and chest. "Let me go! Let me go! My dad will kill you!"

"Do you think I'm worried about that storekeeper? I know who you are. I've seen you around that store. I've watched you come and go, and knew I had to have yuh. Now behave yourself and you won't get hurt."

He put his hand on her shoulder and ran it down the front of her dress. She hit him some more, and screamed again.

George turned his conversation with Gray over in his mind as he walked up the hill to his house. Maybe they should have a bigger jail. It was a mining town and miners were noted for carousing in the saloons on Saturday nights. No. He'd been in other towns with that same kind of situation, and their jails were no bigger. No, there's something else that is happening here. Too many toughs hitting town all at once.

Suddenly, he heard a scream that sounded like it came from down on Main Street. He stopped and listened. There was another one! George ran down the hill toward the center of town. Now, which way to go? It could have come from either direction. He stood trying to hear some other sound that would give him an idea which way to go. Then a third scream came from across the street.

He looked over that way, but couldn't see anything as he ran across the street and started down toward the haberdashery. He had just come from there, and hadn't seen anything unusual, but that was where it sounded like that last scream came from. As he passed the barber shop, he thought he heard sounds coming from the alleyway beside the building. He stopped, and could hear voices back there in the dark.

George drew his pistol and stepped into the gap between the buildings. He stopped to listen and let his eyes adapt to the darkness, and could hear a struggle there further into the gloom. "Who's there? Come out with your hands in the air!"

He could hear a man cursing, then a woman's voice. "Help! Help me!"

George ran on into the dark alleyway and crashed into a man who was getting to his feet. George's rush knocked the man to the ground, and as he fell, he tripped George, who fell on top of the man. George immediately felt the man's hands surround his neck and start choking him.

George punched the man in the face and a couple of times in the stomach, then, he was able to get his arms free enough to knock the man's hands away and get his breath back. This gave him some room to swing his fists, and a couple of sharp blows put the man out and on the ground.

George quickly handcuffed the outlaw, and looked around for the woman. She was sitting on the ground, sobbing. He helped her to her feet, and led her out to the street. "Oh - Miss Gray! Are you all right?"

"Sheriff Menton, I'm so glad you came! That man was----!"

"I know. If you're not hurt, go on home; I'll watch from here until you get there. I'd walk you, but I've got to take care of that hombre in there."

Ruby put her arms around his neck and hugged him. "Thank you, thank you so much!" She turned and ran for the store.

George stood and watched her until she went into the store, then walked back into the alleyway. He then scraped around the ground with his foot until he found the gun that had been knocked out of his hand in the struggle. He picked it up, holstered it, and then, reached down and slapped the outlaw sharply to bring him to, and raised him to his feet. "Move out! One blink of your eye, and I'll gladly use this pistol and finish the job I should have done in the first place."

George took the man into the jail, tried to figure which of the cells had the least number of inmates, and finally saw one man standing in the second cell that he had arrested the night before. He pointed to him as he opened the cell door. "You there, come here."

The man threaded his way over to where George was standing. "You wanted me?"

"Yes, you're free to go, but if I catch you at it again, it'll be for a lot longer time. Now git."

Then he took the cuffs off of the man he had just brought in and pushed him into the full cell. As he turned to go, there was an outcry from the inmates to let them out, and along with that, a great number of them cursing at him.

George said, "When you can behave yourself, you won't be in there. Now, I think I'll go see if I can find some more to throw in there so you won't get lonesome." He left and walked into his office.

Ruby saw her father putting a hat display together on a counter. She ran over to him. "Oh, Daddy, it was terrible! That terrible man!'

"What happened, Ruby? Are you all right?"

"One of those outlaws caught me and pulled me in between some buildings. He knocked me down and tried to kiss me! Then he hit me in the face several times. Sheriff Menton came and knocked him out. Oh, it was awful!

"Well, no more walking out there by yourself. From now, on, if you want to go anywhere, you'll wait until I can go with you. Thank God we have George here now to look after things.

The next morning, George walked down to Susan's for breakfast. It was early, and she was alone. She brought a cup of coffee over to his table.

"Morning, George. What'll it be this morning - oh, don't tell me. Pancakes, bacon and eggs. It's always pancakes and eggs in the morning, and pot roast, mashed potatoes, and onions at night. I can just keep it warmed up and serve it when you come in the door."

George laughed. "That'll do it, except for one other thing. Will you go to the opera house with me tonight?"

"A rough and tough old sheriff would go to a show! I never heard of such a thing."

"Rough and tough old sheriff's will go most anywhere if there's a beautiful woman to go with them."

"With talk like that, how could a lady refuse? I'll be glad to go, George. I haven't been there for a long time. It's silly, but I feel like a sixteen-year-old on her first date." She smiled and said, "You, sir, are an old rascal!" She left to fix his breakfast.

George sat wondering how he had had the nerve to do that, but at the same time, he was darned glad he did. Susan was a very attractive woman and he had been wanting to do that ever since he got here.

The night air was pleasant, as were George's thoughts, as he stepped up to Susan's front door. He knocked, and when she opened the door, she took his breath away. She was beautiful! He had seen her day after day in her working clothes, stray hairs hanging over her face from brushing it away over the cook stove, but now! She was a sight to behold.

Her shining flaxen hair fell to her shoulders, with a bit of curl at the ends. She wore a two-toned green dress that brought out the hazel color of her eyes, with a pearl necklace accentuating the beauty of her complexion. But, most of all, her killer smile that greeted him as he stepped through the door had George tongue-tied.

Susan said, "Come in, George, I'll be with you in a minute." She left through a door at the back of the room.

George looked over the room. It was comfortable-looking. Several large chairs were placed around the walls. There were two large windows and a fireplace, which took up much of the wall space, with a large woven rug in the center of the room that all added to the décor.

Susan came back and walked up to George.

"Well, Sir, are you ready to go?"

"—Uh --yes. Susan, you are beautiful! Uh—yes, let's go."

What was the matter with him? He couldn't think of anything to say. It was a lot easier to talk to a gunslinger with a forty-five staring at him. He held out his arm for her to take and they walked down the sidewalk to the Opera House, George walking on air all the way.

Sitting in the Opera House, George could feel her presence there beside him until it was difficult to concentrate on the show.

When the production was over, and they walked out the door, George asked her, "Would you like to go somewhere and get something to eat?"

She laughed. "You are talking to the owner of a café. I'd rather go there. We can be alone there and not have to try to overcome all the noise from others. I have coffee and rolls at the ready. Let's go there."

When the coffee was heated and the rolls warmed, she brought it all to the table and sat down across from him. "George, I had a wonderful time; thanks for asking me. I haven't been out on a date for years, nor wanted to."

"I can say the same. I never thought I would date again, but you are something else. Can we do it again?"

"You have only to ask."

 # CHAPTER FIFTEEN

Rain was pouring onto the roof when Bart awoke. He felt drug out, and would like to just stay right there in bed. He should get up and tell the crew to take a day off. They had earned it, and there was not much they could do with it raining this hard, anyhow.

He got up and built a fire. Then he walked down to the cook-shack. Carmelita had coffee made. Bart sat down at the table, and she brought a cup to him.

"Senor Bart, I hope you not mad at us for having our own house."

"No. Why would I be mad?"

"I get that man to marry me if we have our own house. Besides, two women not live in same house too good. You be bringing your woman in soon."

"Carmelita, you have been our cook ever since we left Texas. We're getting big enough now that we can afford a cook. You and Al should have your own place, and live your own lives. I'll look for a cook and get him here as soon as I can. You have my thanks for all you've done for these last few years."

"I glad to do it. I like to cook, and I like all the boys."

Al, Slim, Bear and Shorty came through the door, each grabbing a cup of coffee and sitting down at the table.

Slim lifted his cup to Carmelita. "Here's to the best cook in the country. I've jest about starved to death, Carmelita, waitin' to eat some o' your cookin'."

Bart laughed. "Yeah, I noticed - four steaks at a sittin', along with two loaves of bread and three apple pies. I had to get a bank loan to pay his food bill on the trip!"

Slim turned red. "Aw, shecks, a man jest has to eat what he's worth. If yuh do three times as much work as anybody else, yuh should get to eat three times as much grub."

Bart waited until they had finished eating. "Wait a minute before you head out the door. After what we learned in Butte, I think we'd better change some things around here. I want you all to work in twos from now on until this thing is over. Wear your gunbelts all the time and keep your rifles within reach, or at least, where you can get 'em quick."

Slim said, "Boss, do you think they'd come over here t' the ranch? What'd they want with us? We c'd bust 'em in the chops, an' if thet didn't work, I'd sic ol' Roany on 'em!"

"You might have to. I don't think they're main push is here; more than likely it's either the miners or Virginia City, from what the man in Butte said, but we had better be ready in any case. I'm goin' up to town and tell George what we heard. He needs to know. If they do come in force, we may have to go up there and help out. It won't do us any good if that town is run by outlaws."

Five riders were going down the main road ahead of him as Bart rode down to the post office at Alder. He swung in behind them, keeping some distance between them and himself. He followed them up the hill and into the city. They didn't stop or even slow down as they rode up the main street. He watched them continue through town, until he turned off up the side street to the jail.

George was not in the office when Bart went in. The new deputy, Jack Billings, was sitting at the desk, and introduced himself. Bart asked, "Is George around?"

"He went down to the haberdashery and I think he'll be back soon."

Going back out, Bart looked down toward Main Street and saw George coming up the hill toward him. Bart went back into the office, and waited.

George hung his hat on a peg after entering. "Hello, Bart. Guess you've met our new deputy. What brings you to town?"

"George, we were just up at Butte with some cattle, and one of the miners told us that a bunch of owlhoots that were in Butte have moved down to Nevada City. You remember the town down on the river? He said they had it in mind to rob the miners, and take over Virginia City. Thought you should know."

"Well, that explains all the increase of outlaws running around town. It sounds like we'd better get some preparations made, and quick. Are you staying in town?"

"If you need me. We did run into a couple of 'em coming back."

"Let's go down and see Gray. He might have some thoughts on this."

Jim Gray was waiting on a customer when they entered the store. "Be with you fellows in a minute."

When he had finished with his customer, he walked over to where they were standing. "George, Bart, anything the matter?"

Bart told him what they'd found out in Butte. George said, "Jim, I think now is the time we had better get prepared for them. Can you get your council together this afternoon?"

"I think so. Three o'clock all right?"

"That'll do. I'll be around town, and back here at three."

Bart said, "If you don't need me, I have some business to attend to."

Gray grinned. "She's upstairs. Go on up."

Bart took the stairs two at a time and knocked on the door. Ruby opened the door. "Bart! I am so glad to see you. Come in."

He took her in his arms and held her. "I missed you, Ruby. When this mess is over, let's get married."

"What mess?"

"I think there's going to be big trouble. There's a bunch of outlaws down in Nevada City that're going to cause trouble, I think."

"They are already causing trouble. One of them attacked me the other day."

"What happened?"

"One grabbed me and pulled me in between a couple of buildings. Sheriff Menton came in and saved me. It was horrible!"

"Damn! Ruby, don't even go outside until this is all over. It's goin' to be bad, I think. Stay in the store, and don't even stay down there alone. There are a bunch of toughs coming in, and you would be helpless against them."

"I will, Bart. I'm getting scared."

"I think you'll be all right here in the store. We're going to have to do something about them quick. Your father is getting the council together in a little bit to come up with a plan."

He fished in his pocket and came out with a small box. "We've been engaged for some time now, but I never had a ring to give you. I found one in Butte." He reached into the box, pulled out the ring, and put it on her finger.

"Oh, Bart, it's beautiful!" She threw her arms around his neck and kissed him.

"Not nearly as beautiful as you. Aw, Ruby, I love you. I'm tired of waiting. I hope we get this trouble cleared up right away."

Later that afternoon, two of the councilmen were coming into the store as Bart came down the stairs. He took a seat beside them. Within a few minutes, the rest started to file in, followed by Buster and George Menton.

Jim Gray said, "Now that we're all here, I'll ask Bart to fill us in on the news he heard at Butte the other day, but first, I'm sure you all remember George Menton, our new sheriff. He's been busy filling up our jail. I'm glad to report that I've been able to get a deputy for George. His name is Jack Billings."

Bart relayed what they had been told in Butte, and then told about their run-in in Nevada City.

Jim said, "Just the other day Ruby was attacked and drug into a space between a couple of buildings right here on Main Street. Lord only knows what would have happened to her if George hadn't heard her, and rescued her. It looks like the time has come when we've got to take drastic action. George has the saloons closing at one A.M., and that has helped some, but if they're coming in with fifty, or more, outlaws, we are in big trouble. George, you tell us what to do and we'll back you up."

George sat looking at the floor and pulling the corners of his mustache. "No one knows what they're going to do. With a bunch like that, it might depend on how much liquor they've been drinking, or what some one of them thinks is a good idea. From what Bart says, they plan to hit the miners, and also plan to take over the town. My guess is they'll hit the miners down in the gulch first. The miners will be completely unorganized, and they can just come in quietly and take each miner as they come up the creek and steal his gold. Then, when they reach the town, they can come in over the ridge and down into the town from above. At least, that's how I would do it. We won't know until we see the whites of their eyes.

"Buster, when we leave here, line up all the vigilantes you can get. I understand many of them are miners. Warn all of the miners that they may be coming any time and to have their guns and ammunition ready. When the time comes, lead them down into the gulch, and pick up every miner you can and move on down the creek. Jim, get every townsman that you can get with a gun, and meet here. I'll go with you and we'll march right down the hill on the main road. If we can time it right, we'll catch them just as they're leaving the road to go into the gulch.

"Bart, you bring your crew up the gulch from the river. We'll hem 'em in and hopefully be able to convince 'em to give up when they see that they don't have a great numbers advantage. Just be careful you're not shooting across them and hitting our own boys.

"This isn't going to be a picnic. I'm sure that many of them are gunslingers, and some of us may get shot. It's just a matter of doing it on our own terms, or letting them get us piecemeal over time. Now, timing is the problem. How are we going to find out when they make their move? It'll be a lot easier to catch 'em in the open than to try to root 'em out of those houses in Nevada City."

Jim said, "I'll get someone to take his horse and stay at the post office in Alder. He can see them coming up the road from Nevada City, and he can ride up and warn us. We'll ring the church bell to warn everybody to get together. Then go from there."

Bart said, "I'll have one man on watch from the ranch. We'll follow them and when they get to the flat, we'll cross over to the creek and intercept them there, if they come that way."

George said, "All right, it sounds like that is the best we can do. Better get the lookouts on the job right now, and everybody have your guns and a lot of ammunition ready to go in a minute. It may even be tonight they come."

Susan had four meals cooking on the grill. The makings of a salad for each were on the counter. She took out a knife and started to work on them. When that was finished, she put the salad material into four bowls and took them out to the customers herself, since the waitress was clearing some tables.

As Susan looked around, she saw George sitting at a table at the back of the room. Her heart gave a jump. What's the matter with you, old girl? You are too old for that sort of thing. Nevertheless, a smile grew on her face and she walked over to his table.

"Hello, George. You here for supper?"

"Yeah, and a bottle of your best bourbon."

"You'll have to go to another establishment for that, but I have a bowl of delicious pot roast with mashed potatoes and onions in the warming oven, just waiting for a certain sheriff I know. You hang on and it'll be out in a jiffy, with a cup of coffee. Hard day?"

"Not so far, but the day ain't over yet, either. Susan, I want to talk to you before I go."

"All right. When I get these folks over there fed, I'll come around. Besides that, I've got a treat for you."

"You are a treat for me, but what are you talkin' about?"

"It's a recipe of my mother's. I always looked forward to it. Strawberry-rhubarb pie. I hope you'll like it."

The waitress brought George's pot roast dinner and he was nearly finished with it by the time Susan came back to his table. She sat down across the table from him with a piece of pie for both of them and a pot of coffee. "A warm-up on that coffee?"

"Yes, thanks. Susan, I want you to make me a promise."

"What is it, George? I will if I can."

"Promise me you won't go out on the street alone again until I say it's all right."

"I have to go out to get home. How would I do that?"

"I'll be over every night at quitting time to walk you home. You wait until I get here."

"What's the matter? Is something wrong?"

"The Gray girl was attacked yesterday. Luckily, I heard her scream. There are supposed to be a lot more toughs around town right away. I don't want you hurt."

"Is she allright?

"Yes, she seemed fine, a little shookup."

"Oh, I'm so glad. All right, I'll wait for you, but I don't want you to go to all that trouble."

"It'll be no trouble for me to walk the prettiest girl in town home."

"You keep that kind of talk up and you'll fair turn my head."

"I hope so. Don't forget. These birds are a mean bunch from all I hear. And, Susan, that's the best pie I ever ate."

Birch Morton looked over the group in front of him. They were all milling around in the abandoned warehouse. They were a tough bunch. His big problem was going to be keeping control of them. He had been on the outlaw trail for a lot of years and never seen a tougher-looking bunch all in one place in his life. It looked to him as if there were at least fifty of them here in the building. He climbed up on an empty box and fired his pistol at the ceiling.

"You all came here with the idea of makin' a haul from the miners over in Alder Gulch. We've held off until there's enough of us to walk through there without much resistance. There's about fifty or so of us now, and tonight, we'll make the run.

"The money you get from this first raid will only be chicken feed to what we'll get eventually. When we get through the gulch and have cleaned the miners out that are in there, we're goin' to cut up the left side of the gulch, go over that ridge and move into Virginia City. We're gonna take it over lock, stock and barrel.

"We don't wanta do any more killin' than we can help. We're gonna' live off these miners and townsfolks from now on. We'll own the stores and the storekeepers'll work for us. The miners'll have to come to our stores for their supplies. The storekeepers'll give us the profits from their stores.

"Sam Divers, over there on the end. Sam, raise your hand. There. Sam and I will lead you through town. We'll leave one or two of you at each store and you'll stay there holding it down 'til we have the owners under control. After it calms down, we'll bring them into line and set up a procedure for them to pay us the profits every day.

"When we come into town, we'll go down the hill to Main Street. Sam'll go up the hill to the right, and I'll go to the left. We'll each take half of you with us and put you in the stores. Remember, don't kill anyone you don't have to, but if you need to, shoot. We'll start early mornin'; that should put us in the gulch just before daylight - just in time to catch the miners in their nightclothes."

Someone in the back said, "What about that new sheriff they have? I heard he is a stem-winder."

"Look around you. There's enough firepower here to take on the army. What's one man goin' to do?"

CHAPTER SIXTEEN

Just before dawn, the watchman at the Alder post office heard the sound of many horses' hooves on the rocky road. He ran to his horse and was off at a gallop up the hill toward Virginia City. His first stop was the church. He rushed inside and reached for the rope that rang the bell. He pulled it vigorously, and the bell pealed loudly, waking the entire town.

Buster grabbed his rifle, buckled on his gun-belt, and headed over the ridge and into the gulch. Some of the miners had heard the bell and were getting dressed when he got there. Clint Basset's tent was just up the creek from where he came over the hill. Buster went there first.

"Hey, Clint, the time's come! They rang the bell. How many men did you round up?"

"Four of the old bunch of vigilantes is all that's still around. They're ready to go. Maybe we can pick up a few more on the way down. Are they coming up the creek?"

"Don't know. The sheriff and the townspeople are goin' down the road to meet 'em. He wants us to go down the creek and meet 'em at the flat, if they come that way."

"Hang on 'til I get muh boots on, and we'll pick up the others as we go. They're all further down the creek."

The two men worked their way down the creek, stopping at every placer site as they went. The four vigilantes came with them, and some of the others agreed to follow after they got dressed and retrieved their guns. Buster told them all to meet at the bottom of the gulch, just before the canyon leveled out onto the flat.

George Menton rushed to the haberdashery when he heard the bell. Jim Gray came out of the building just as he arrived. Both men were armed with pistols and rifles. Storekeepers, shop owners, and others came in bunches to where the two were waiting. George estimated there were around twenty men when they stopped coming.

"Men, we're goin' right down the road. No one make any noise. Surprise is our best medicine. When we approach that crowd, I want you to stop. I'll go on to meet 'em and see if we can settle this peaceably. No one shoot until I do. If they do move into the gulch, we'll just have to surround 'em and make 'em give up."

They moved down the hill on the main road, George and Jim Gray leading the group.

The ridge between the road and Alder Gulch ran out into a flat filled with sagebrush, juniper and, closer to the water, cottonwood and willow. George stopped when he reached the flat and dispersed the men on both sides of the road. He and Jim Gray each took a side of the road and found some cover to stand behind. Then they prepared to wait until the outlaws reached them.

Buster looked over his five vigilantes. There were about that many more miners they had picked up as they worked their way down the gulch. Many of the miners they had contacted on the way had disbelieved his story about the outlaws approach.

Buster led the way quietly, knowing that they could come face to face with the outlaws at any moment. When they reached the flat, he stopped and placed what men he had in strategic spots on each side of the creek. He climbed a short way up the hillside on the far side of the creek where he could command a view of the flat.

He could see Clint on the far bank, and three of his men just below him. The ridge between Alder Creek and the road ended just below where Clint had stationed his men. If the outlaws were going to come up the creek to get at the miners, they would have to come between where he was and Clint's position. They should be able to catch the outlaws in a cross-fire, with only minimum danger to themselves. Now, it was a waiting game.

The Ruby River Ranch crew hustled up the creek from the west. When they reached the flat, Bart led them up the hillside on the far side of the creek, and picked out strategic spots where they could look up the flat toward the gulch. This would place them in a position where they could fire down on the outlaws, should they come this way. They were each behind fairly good-sized boulders where they would have reasonably good protection.

Bart took the position closer to the direction the outlaws would likely come from. Then he sat down and watched the flat. This was not going to be any Saturday night social. The flat below him was covered with brush of some kind. Willows, juniper, and sage covered most of the flat, and were fairly thick. If the outlaws got into that, it would be hard to see them and to know who you were shooting at, or who was shooting at you.

Waiting was difficult, especially when you knew the outcome could be so drastic. He checked his rifle and his pistol again to be sure they were ready to go. That was the third time he had done that - did he think the shells would have spilled out, or something? Get hold of yourself, Bart Madison! It was just that the thought of the fifty-or-so gunslingers from Nevada City coming at the four of them was a little overwhelming.

Birch Morton turned in his saddle and looked at the gang of outlaws he had put together. It looked like a young army! There was no way that bunch of townspeople and the sleepy miners along the gulch were going to even slow them down. The townspeople were storekeepers that probably didn't even know how to load a gun, let alone use it, and they were going to catch the miners before breakfast. This was going to be a piece of cake!

He looked over at Sam Divers riding beside him. "The flat ends just ahead. We'll peel off the road when we get there, and work our way across the flat. It's brushy enough that we can get all the way to the creek where the miners're working without anyone bein' the wiser. We'll leave the horses there in the flat, and go up the creek on foot. We can be quieter that way and surprise 'em before they know we're in the country.

"When we get to the creek, we need to scatter out and start movin' on the miners. Catch 'em before they know we're there and take their guns and their gold, and move on. When we get far enough up the creek that we're even with the town, we need to get together again, and then we'll go over the ridge and down through the town. What th--!"

As he was talking to Divers, a man stepped out onto the road. He held up a hand. "Turn around - this's as far as you're goin'!"

Morton pulled back on the reins. He looked at the man. "Damn! It can't be. That looks like George Menton! What's he doin' here?" He hadn't expected this. He looked over at Divers. "Menton! Did you know he was here?"

"What difference does that make? Like yuh said, what can one man do?"

"I don't know, I just know that he's done a lot in Texas, and Oklahoma, and even in Kansas. I don't like this. I didn't know the sheriff that guy was talkin' about was George Menton!"

"What're you goin' to do?"

"Get ready. We'll go into the flat shootin'. Even George Menton can't stand up to that. Get ready to draw your guns and run. He must have backing. Wait 'til I shoot." He looked back at where George was standing. "Is that you, George?"

"Well, Birch Morton. What are you doin' outside of a Texas jail?"

"A little sideline work. You alone, George?"

"I've got an army behind me. Now, you have only one choice and that is to turn around, Birch. You're goin' no further."

"You're wrong, George." His hand dropped swiftly to his gun. Before his gun was up to level, bullets were beating into his vest. George Menton stood with a smoking gun. Morton's horse shied at the gunfire and crashed into Divers' horse. Divers shot went into the air. Menton stepped back to the rock he had been standing behind, and kept a steady round of shots into the outlaw group. A fusillade erupted from both sides of the road where the townspeople had deployed, emptying a number of outlaw saddles. The remaining toughs rode for the cover of the brush-covered flat, shooting as they rode.

Divers shouted, "Get together at the creek!"

Bullets flew back and forth between the townspeople near the road, and the outlaws fleeing through the brush. Limbs were torn off the trees, bullets that bounced off the rocks sang as they ricocheted through the air, and thudded as they found their marks in trees, the earth, and the bodies of the outlaws.

It was general chaos among the outlaws, riding pell-mell among the trees and brush on the flat. Divers kept yelling at them to regroup and meet at the creek.

George said to himself: Here we go again. This is a bunch of Texas towns and Oklahoma all over again. There, I had some lawmen with me, sometimes; this time, it's a few storekeepers against fifty or so gunmen. Maybe if we can keep 'em running toward the miners and cowboys, they can cut the odds down a little.

He followed the outlaws into the brushy flat, motioning the townspeople forward.

General chaos erupted. The flat, overgrown with alder, willows, sagebrush, and filled with piles of shifted gravel from the mining, caused the outlaws to lose their sense of direction. Everyone was firing their guns in every direction when they would see a bush move or hear a noise. They rode their horses helter-skelter through the brush, shooting as they went.

George rallied his men and followed the outlaws onto the flat. They kept up a steady barrage of bullets, keeping the outlaws on the run, and forcing them to ride toward the creek and to the ambush waiting for them by Buster and the miners. The constant pressure from the townspeople would deprive them of a chance to regroup and start fighting back. The outlaws fired back, but having to stop, turn and shoot behind them, or fire over their shoulders, their fire was mostly ineffective. They pushed on for the creek.

Divers rallied his men as best he could as they reached the creek. "Come on. Follow me. We'll find positions up the creek and ambush 'em as they follow us."

His men gathered behind him, and they started up the creek. As they rounded the first bend into the gulch, there was a wall of fire from the miners on the hillside across the creek, and another from the vigilantes on the ridge. Outlaws were mowed down like grass, and those left beat a hasty retreat.

Divers led the few men he had left on the run downstream. Buster and the vigilantes came charging down the hillside and from the ridge to follow them, and George and the townspeople were fast closing in from the roadside.

Divers saw no choice but to run on downstream and try to escape that direction. If they went up the steep hillside to the south, they would be sitting ducks from the shooters on the flat. There was no cover there that would let them move without being seen. Menton and the townspeople were closing in on them from the north, and they couldn't face that barrage from up the canyon. Their only choice was to try to get away downstream to the west.

How in the billy blue did they get in this fix? Birch had said how easy this was going to be! Yeah, all they had to do was walk up the creek and catch the miners in their sleep! He yelled out, "Follow me. We'll go out this way."

Bart heard the firing from the road and the flat, and then from upstream. He checked the ranch hands. All of them were in place and standing with their rifles at the ready. There must be a lot of the outlaws in the mix. The number of gunshots he had been hearing had to come from a lot of guns. It was almost like a steady roar. Well, however many came down that creek, Ruby River was going to do their best to stop them. He checked the loads in his rifle for the third time. It was still ready to go.

Divers led his men at a gallop, and pulled away from the gunfire from the gulch. There was no fire from Menton now; maybe it was going to work. It seemed they had left their enemies behind. He started to relax just a little. It seemed they had made it.

Suddenly, a line of fire came from the rocks above. The Ruby River crew opened up from behind a row of boulders on the hill above them. Once again, his numbers were getting smaller by the second. He had to turn back once again.

The outlaws were in turmoil. It seemed no matter where they went there was an army of guns waiting for them.

Bart and the Ruby River crew kept a steady fire down into the roiling mass of outlaws on the flat below them. Bullets were flying toward them, as well. He looked over to his left at Slim, who was kneeling behind a boulder, shooting down at the flat. "Slim, how's your ammunition holdin' out?"

I got 'nuff to fill the magazine again, then I'm gonna hafta cut me a billy club and go after 'em. I niver seen so many catawhompers all in a herd in muh life!"

"I'm about in the same fix. Better conserve your shells. Take your time and be sure of each shot. We don't want to run out."

There was a small clearing that bordered the creek that they had to cross. Divers halted as he came to it. He only had a handful of men left. They had to get across the clearing, and quickly. The shooters downstream were closing on them. He shouted. "Run for it. We'll hole up in the brush on the other side, and get 'em as they cross the clearing comin' after us."

Divers rushed into the clearing, followed by about twenty of his men. As he reached the middle of the clearing, Buster and the vigilantes came out of the brush ahead of them. Divers stopped. They had to try for the road! He turned in that direction, started that way and came face to face with George Menton and the townspeople. Then Bart and the Ruby Ranch crew came into the clearing from the west. They were surrounded.

George walked over toward him, as Divers turned around in every direction. He had nowhere to go! He faced George. "Stay back, lawman!

You may have us surrounded, but you'll never see us in jail. I'll nail you before you take another step."

George said, "Divers, you were a big man in Oklahoma, you and that crew you led. You killed a lot of innocent people, and a few gunmen, and got yourself a reputation. This is where it ends. Tell your men to throw down their guns, and come peaceable."

"You'll never take me alive, lawman. We'll mow you down, and those storekeepers there with yuh."

George kept on walking, his gun pointed at the ground.

Divers said again. "Menton, stop! I'm faster than you. You'll not see another sunrise."

George kept walking. He held out his hand and kept looking Divers in the eye, unblinking.

Divers stared back. "Stop! I'll kill you. Stop!"

George walked right up to the man, looking him in the eye. He reached up and took the man's gun. Diver's shoulders drooped in defeat. George reached around for his handcuffs and slapped them on Diver's wrists. Everybody moved in on the outlaws and divested them of their arms. It was over!

They sat the outlaws down on the ground, and George looked around the group standing there. "How many have we lost, or are hurt? Take inventory."

Jim Gray looked around at the townspeople. "Jeff Pierson took a bullet in his leg back at the road, and Salty has a wound in his side. Otherwise, we're all right, I think."

Buster said, "We lost a miner in that first go-around; otherwise, we're fine."

Bart said, "We're good, too. No injuries."

Slim spoke up, "Wal, muh father's oldest boy jest lost forty years when them shorthorns come roustin' through the brush. Ah lef' muh fingerprints on the bar'l o' muh rifle right then."

George grinned. "You all did great! Let's get our wounded taken care of and get these ranahans up to the jail. We'll have to send a party down here to search this flat for dead, and bury them.

A miner stepped up. "Leave that to us. It's the least we can do after you kept those outlaws from robbing us, or worse. We have the tools, and glad to do it."

Salty Borden raised a hand. "There's free drinks at the Golden Goose all day!"

Bart sent his crew back home and then helped herd the outlaws back up the hill to the jail. George cleared out enough of the occupants of the cells with minor infractions, to make room for the outlaws. When the cell doors clanked shut, a thin, pale individual worked his way to the front. Jim recognized him. "Jackson, what are you doing in there?"

"He threw me in here for no reason at all. You've got to get me out! They're going to kill me in here."

Jim turned to George. "What has he done?"

"Actually, he's the brains behind all of this. He contacted the right people in Butte, told them about the miners, and the possibility of gleaning their gold from them, and then he has been directing operations of the outlaw bunch ever since. I kept noticing these characters going into the drug store up there all the time, so I followed a couple of them in, and pretended to be looking for something to buy. I was able to hear enough to find out what they were doing. I thought this would be a more suitable quarters for him."

Jim said, "I imagine that he was eager to have them take over the town. He has more or less been in disfavor around here since he ran off from Ruby when they were dating, and left her to the toughs that confronted them. Good riddance!"

"Yeah, while I was standing there he was telling two of them that he would be the mayor of the town, and he would make them the police chief, and tax collector. He probably had that desertion gnawing at him for a long time, and this was his chance to make a hero of himself."

The group shook hands all around and left on their separate ways, some to the Golden Goose.

Bart walked with Jim Gray down to the haberdashery. Ruby was upstairs in her room when Bart knocked on the door. She rushed into his arms when she saw him.

"Bart, thank goodness! I've been so worried. Is it all over?"

"It's over. Ruby, I was thinking when we were sitting there waiting for the outlaws, that one bullet could end your life just like that. It would be all over. Life's too short. Let's get married right now."

"Me, too. While I was waiting, I realized what a fool I've been to keep putting things off. I'm ready!"

He kissed her. "I'll go get the preacher."

"Oh, no, you don't. I'm not in that much of a hurry. We're going to have a nice church wedding. I didn't put that much work in on my wedding dress, not to show it to the world. How about the first of the month? That'll give you two weeks to get ready."

"You mean, it'll give you two weeks to get ready. I'm ready right now."

She smiled and hugged him. "I guess you could say that. Bart, I'm so happy! We've waited so long, and I know it is my fault that we did. Let's go down and tell my folks."

Mabel Gray rushed over and hugged her daughter. "Oh, baby, I'm so glad!" Then she turned and threw her arms around Bart's neck. "Welcome to our family. I'm so glad it's you." Then she went back to her daughter, and started talking about the wedding.

Jim Gray, who had been standing back watching, walked over to Bart and held out his hand. "Congratulations, Bart. I have to tell you, when she first started going with you I had some big reservations about her getting too chummy with a cattleman. I've seen some of those ranch wives come in looking like a worn-out shoe, and old before their time. But, after getting to know you, I couldn't be happier. Welcome to the family."

Bart said, "Thanks Jim. I love her very much, and I intend to keep her happy, and well fed. I intended to ask your blessing before I proposed, but things kind of got away from us."

CHAPTER SEVENTEEN

The day finally arrived. Bart felt more nervous than if he were facing down a notorious killer. He got out his best suit, and laid it on the bed. It looked all right. He shaved and went down to the cook shack. Carmelita looked up as he entered.

"Senor Bart, are you all right? You look a little pale." She smiled and brought him a cup of coffee, followed quickly by a platter of pancakes, bacon and eggs. "Eat hearty, you'll need lots of energy today. Tomorrow, you'll be Senor Ruby!" She laughed and went back to her stove.

The crew came in, everyone joshing Bart about losing his independence and looking forward to a hen-pecked life from now on. He talked to them about how the barbeque was coming along, and plans for the reception here on the ranch after the ceremony.

Carmelita, said, "You leave them do their work. They fix everything up good. You come with me. I fix your suit up fine. You got to look good!"

She followed him into his room, and picked up the suit. "This is terrible. You no get married in this!"

She took the suit back to her room, picked the lint and other unwanted items off the cloth, brushed it, and then pressed it. Then she brought it back into his room. "There. Now you no get it dirty before you married!"

Bart changed into his suit, tied his unfamiliar tie, and walked into the living room. His crew was already there, dressed out in their finest. He hardly recognized them in their finery. "Is this my crew? You look like a bunch of dudes."

Slim said, "I think thet skillet is callin' th' kettle black. Yuh'd better know, Boss, I didn't put this monkey suit on fer yew. It was fer thet purty little gal you're marryin'."

Al bowed from the waist. "Your carriage awaits, your lordship. Your footmen are at the ready."

Carmelita came into the room. She was dressed in a long, pale-blue, flowing dress. Bart had never seen her dressed up before. She was a beauty. She walked over, threw her arms around Bart, and kissed him on the cheek. "You are a good man, Senor Bart. I glad you marry her."

Al grinned. "Hey, watch that, Bart. That's the one I'm gonna marry. Let's get this show on the road, before he starts takin' a likin' to my gal."

The buggy was shined to a fare-thee-well, the horse combed down and brushed until he glistened, and there was a blanket over the seats.

Bart stepped out the door and walked over to the shiny rig. "Do I have to take my boots off before I get in?"

Carmelita came out with a bunch of wild flowers she had picked, walked up to the horse and tied them upright to the front of the horse's bridle. "See, Senor Bart, the horse, he look pretty, too, for the bride."

The wagon was in a similar state, with a blanket on the bed where the hands would sit. Al lifted Carmelita into the wagon seat, and the crew crawled onto the bed. The Ruby River crew left for Virginia City.

The church was filled to capacity with flowers, pictures, draperies and more, with lady friends of Mabel Gray scurrying around to make everything right. Some early comers were already seated, wanting to have a good seat where they could see and hear. George Menton came in through the front door, with Susan on his arm, both dressed in their finest, and took seats near the front of the church.

The preacher came in, and stood at the altar, shuffling his papers and getting his thoughts in order. Bart came in with his crew and took their places at the side of the preacher. Al stood next to him, then Slim, and then Buster. Shorty, and Carmelita's father took their seat in the front row.

At this point, Bear, who had been assigned the job of escort, came down the aisle with Ruby's mother, who was wearing a lovely, pale-yellow dress, and seated her, with a bow and a proud smile, on the front row. He then took his seat beside Shorty.

They stood waiting, watching the door to the side room at the back, through which Bart hoped that Ruby would soon be coming. The lady pianist came into the room, went to the piano, arranged her music, and then began to play.

The longer they stood there the more nervous Bart became. The church was filled with townspeople, miners, and Bart didn't know who else. He didn't know there were that many people in the county. What could be happening? Was Ruby even here? What could be taking so long? He looked at the preacher. He seemed unconcerned enough, just stood there going through his book, and some papers.

On his other side, Al, Buster, and Slim were talking about something that didn't sound like it had anything to do with the wedding. How could they all be so calm? He felt in his pocket. Yep, the ring was still in there.

The side door finally opened. At last, here she comes! No, it was a little girl with a basket. She came slowly down the aisle reaching into the basket and taking out some flower petals which she spread out over the aisle as she walked down it. When she reached where they all were standing, she smiled at Bart, and then took a seat in the second row of seats beside her mother.

Now, surely Ruby would be coming out. What was taking so long? Another long waiting period with nothing happening. He looked over at Buster, Al and Slim. They seemed entirely unconcerned. They were talking about the new forty-five that Colt was selling. How could they be talking about a gun at a time like this?

He kept his eyes on that door. Finally, it opened slowly. Now, maybe this was it. A little girl in a pretty new pink dress came out of the side room and ran up to the piano. She whispered something to the pianist and then took a seat near the front of the room.

The pianist, with gusto, broke into, 'Here Comes the Bride', and the door to the room opened again. Ginny came in wearing a dress of the same pale-blue as the one Carmelita was wearing, followed by another long-time friend of Ruby's, Sally Summers, and then Carmelita. All of them dressed alike.

Next, Jim Gray, resplendent in a new grey suit, emerged with Ruby on his arm. She looked like a dream from heaven, Bart thought. How did he ever get so lucky? He heard Slim say, "Gol Dang, if she ain't th' peach o' the crop!" Bart couldn't have agreed more.

Bart stood watching as Jim Gray and Ruby slowly walked down the aisle. Her dress was a white cloud of lace and satin, her veil flowed from a crown of flowers on her shining hair, which she wore up in soft curls, tendrils curling around her radiant, smiling face. His thoughts bounced back and forth between how beautiful she was, and how he wished she would hurry.

When she stepped up beside him, Jim kissed her cheek and placed her hand on Bart's arm, then, sat down beside his wife in the front row. Bart and Ruby smiled into each other's eyes, then, turned to face the preacher. He started through the ceremony.

After they said their 'I do's', the preacher asked for the ring and Bart dug into his pocket. It wasn't there! He dug deeper, panic hitting him. He took his hand out of his pocket and looked at it and there was no ring! How could that be? He dug in again, with no better results. What did he do now? His heart sank into his boots. He looked around at Al. Al smiled. "Did you check your other pocket?"

Bart put his hand in the other pocket, and there was the ring. He jerked it out, his face very red, and placed the ring on Ruby's left hand. The preacher said, "And now, by the power vested in me by the Territory of Montana, I pronounce you man and wife. You may kiss the bride."

Bart gathered Ruby into his arms, kissed her heartily, tucked her arm proudly through his, and walked with her down the aisle, followed by the wedding party. Then, everyone came crowding around the couple, congratulating them, and all talking at once.

Slim walked across to where Bart and Ruby were standing in the receiving line, and when he reached them, said, "I been waitin' here for longer'n it takes fer a tree to grow to kiss this little filly, now I'm not gonna miss the chanct."

Ruby laughed, "You just come right here and get it, Slim."

The rest followed suit.

The preacher finally got everyone's attention again. "I have been asked to announce that there will be a barbeque at the Ruby River Ranch, just across the river from the Alder post office. The beef has been simmering on a pole for hours, and the hog nearly as long. There is plenty for everyone. Everyone is invited. Bring your best appetite".

After an hour's talking with the crowd, Bart and Ruby ran to the waiting buggy. Bart lifted her to the seat, went around the buggy, got in, and slapped the reins, urging the horse into a fast trot. Cans, bottles, and other various kinds of things that would make a lot of noise were attached on strings to the back of the buggy, and got everyone's attention as they drove down the street.

Bart swore he could smell the meat cooking on the spit as they came up the hill to the house. He drove up to the buildings, jumped out, tied the horse to the hitch rack, then took Ruby in his arms and packed her through the door and into the house. He set her down, and kissed her gently. "Welcome home, Mrs. Madison."

"Thank you, Mr. Madison. It's really happened, hasn't it, Bart? I can hardly believe it! I'm so happy. I think I had better pinch myself, to be sure."

"Me, too, Sweetheart. Now, give me another big kiss and then we had better go about our ranch duties. I'll follow up on the kiss tonight."

"Ranch duties? What are you talking about?"

"Now that you're a rancher's wife, you need to start acting like one. I bought you some Levis, a shirt, and a vest that're on our bed, and there's a pair of boots on your side. We need to go out and greet our guests."

"Ruby smiled, "Oh, so you're picking out my clothes and even which side of the bed is mine?"

"Well, now that you own a great big ranch, you've got to look the part. You don't want your hands to think you're some kind of tenderfoot, or something. Besides, I thought you wouldn't want to get your wedding dress dirty, your daughter might want to wear it. As to the boots, I'll move them to the other side, if you want."

"You think you're so smart! I will get changed—right after I quit strangling you. You are an overbearing scoundrel, but I do love you, and I will try to put up with your shortcomings." She was smiling broadly as he led her into the bedroom.

Beef sizzling as it was cut off the steer, and large pieces of pork from the roasting hog were filling everyone's plate. Lots of beer and other liquid drinks were there waiting, along with salads, beans, potatoes, pies and other pastries rounding out the menu. Everyone was laughing, talking, and having a good time. The children who weren't eating were playing a chasing game. Bart and Ruby were beset with people coming to them with congratulations and good wishes. A table that had been set up for the purpose was overflowing with gifts.

The yard was filling up by the minute. Wagons, buggies and horses were everywhere, people were still crossing the river and coming up the hill, miners were coming in on foot and everyone joined in the festivities when they reached the top of the hill.

Slim stood back, waiting for his chance. Finally, he saw that they were alone and made his way over to them. "Miss Ruby, Uh—Mrs. Madison, Ah'm sure glad you're comin' here to live. This place sure needs some purty'n up. A bunch o' ol' hayseeds been hangin' around here long enough.

These old eyes have jest been hankerin' for somethin' pretty to look at for a long time." Slim reached out and hugged her.

"I'm glad to be here, Slim. I'm looking forward to being here with all of you. Bart has told me about you many times."

Jim Gray sat down on a log next to George Menton. "George, haven't had a chance to tell you thanks for cleaning up that gang of cutthroats. You did a great job. Not only that, you've made the town fairly safe again, and I think it will only get better."

"It wasn't me that did that. The whole town, the miners, and even the Ruby Ranch boys did the work."

"Of course, but it never would have happened if you hadn't put the plan together, and just having you lead it, put everything into perspective for those outlaws. You laid down the law in such a manner that they couldn't overcome it. They didn't even have the nerve to confront you, with fifty men behind them!"

"A lot of law enforcement is getting your bluff in first."

"Well, come on with me, something I want to show you." He reached into his buggy, and pulled out a long, wrapped package. "The City wanted you to have this."

George unwrapped the package. A beautiful bamboo fish pole came out. It was just like the one that the Indians had taken from him! "Bart told me that you had lost yours to the Indians, and what a store you set by it. I hope that it comes near replacing the one you lost."

A tear started to form in George's eyes. "I can't thank you enough! I thought that when I lost my other one, I would never find another like it. It could catch more fish than there's stars in the sky. Thank you so much. You folks have been so kind to me. I'll never forget it."

Jim led him over to one to the wagons. He climbed up on it and held his hand to George to follow him. Jim stood up and faced the crowd, then pulled his pistol and shot into the air. The crowd grew quiet. And Jim started.

"Ladies and Gents. Most of you know George Menton, and for you who don't, this man here beside me is him. George has cleaned up half the wild towns in the west, and now he has ours. We want to show our appreciation for what he has done." There was loud clapping and yelling. "We would have soon been back in the same condition we were in when we had the rogue sheriff if it hadn't been for George.

"As a token of our appreciation, the Ruby Ranch has donated a fine quarter-horse, and to go with it, the city has commissioned Bill Baxter to make a hand-tooled saddle and bridle for it. Many of you may have seen the midnight oil burning in his shop lately." He looked around. "Al."

Al came out of the barn, leading a fine bay quarter-horse with a beautifully tooled saddle and bridle, and led it up to the wagon. There was another round of applause from the crowd.

Jim continued. "Also, a new suit of clothes from the haberdashery, a new Henry rifle from the hardware, a year's drinking tab from the Red Garter, and a year's meal ticket from Susan's Café. Another round of applause.

Slim spoke up where everyone could hear. "An' the food is jest th' down payment." A laugh erupted from the crowd who had been seeing George and Susan walking around town together for some time.

Jim said, "George, any words for the folks?"

George stood twirling the ends of his mustache. "When Bart came to me about this job, I turned him down. I thought I had had enough of fighting bad men, and many times without the help of anyone from town. He convinced me that you would back me up, and with a great deal of reluctance, I accepted. I couldn't have done it without you. You all showed a lot of backbone. I am glad I came. I thank you for backing me up, and all of this."

"What now, George? You've cleaned up the town. Are you going to stay? We surely want you to."

George looked over to where Susan was standing with Bart and Ruby. He caught her eye, and smiled. She returned the smile, and he continued. "I've batted around this old world for a lot of years, and I've seen the good and the bad everywhere. Now, I've heard the fishin' is pretty darned good here, and I think this's where I'll put down my roots."

ABOUT THE AUTHOR

Rod Scurlock was born on a ranch in western Washington. He served on a gunboat in the Pacific in WWII. He worked with ranchers, and with Indians during his working career in the United States Department of agriculture and in the Department of the Interior, Bureau of Indian Affairs. He is an avid outdoorsman, and has worked as a natural resources consultant in the State of Idaho. He and his wife Ruth have two children.

Books written by Rod Scurlock include: *Outfitter, Ruby River Ranch,* and *Sparrow,* all published by Borderline Publishing.

Printed in the United States
By Bookmasters